LAKE OF SECRETS

CASSANDRA O'SULLIVAN SACHAR

"This was beautifully written. I loved the pacing and how the story unfolded. The author gave really nice depth to our female MC in a very short amount of pages. If you're looking for a slow-burn who-done-it YA mystery, I highly recommend. Even if you're not a fan of YA, I would still recommend reading this. Truly, it didn't read too much like a YA novel while maintaining appropriateness for the target demographic. Thoroughly enjoyed this one."

ARC Team Review

"I rather enjoyed this as a change to my usual horror. This author is good at weaving all the hints together to the point that all the loose ends are tied up nicely. It will make you wonder why you didn't realise who did what earlier."

ARC Team Review

"This is a beautifully done, slow burn, supernatural YA mystery featuring Callie, a very relatable and smart teenager as the main character, whose quite disciplined and solidly structured personality allows her to solve, step-by-step, a pregnant teen's baffling drowning in a local lake seventy years ago...This slow pace is coupled by a tight and precisely structured plot, whose resolution involves everything that's gone before, from the interesting portrayal of 1940s prejudices about pregnant teens to school friendships and betrayals. The ending provides a very satisfying closure, and repays the time invested by providing hope and stengthening the reader's sense of justice—both greatly appreciated attributes of YA fiction today."

Goodreads Review

ALSO BY CASSANDRA O'SULLIVAN SACHAR

Close the Door
Darkness There But Something Else
Keeper of Corpses
The Hidden Diary

ALSO BY HORRORSMITH PUBLISHING

The Devil Came Down the Mountain
Still, Dark Places
Dark Things Crawl Out
What We Do in Secret
Lake of Secrets
Haint Blue
The Taste of Tiny Bones
A Light on the Bayou
Haunted Halls
Their Hearses
Three Garden Village
Hidden Children
By the Pale Light of Illuminated Bone
Angie Baby
Crepuscular

LAKE OF SECRETS

A Young Adult Mystery

CASSANDRA O'SULLIVAN SACHAR

HORRORSMITH PUBLISHING

An Imprint of Horrorsmith Publishing

For information about special discounts for bulk purchases, please contact Horrorsmith Publishing at lsmith@horrorsmithpublishing.com.

Cover Design by The Cover Collection
Editing by Lyndsey Smith, Horrorsmith Editing
Interior Illustrations by Amanda Bergloff and Lyndsey Smith
Interior Formatting by Lyndsey Smith

ISBN 978-1-967163-93-9

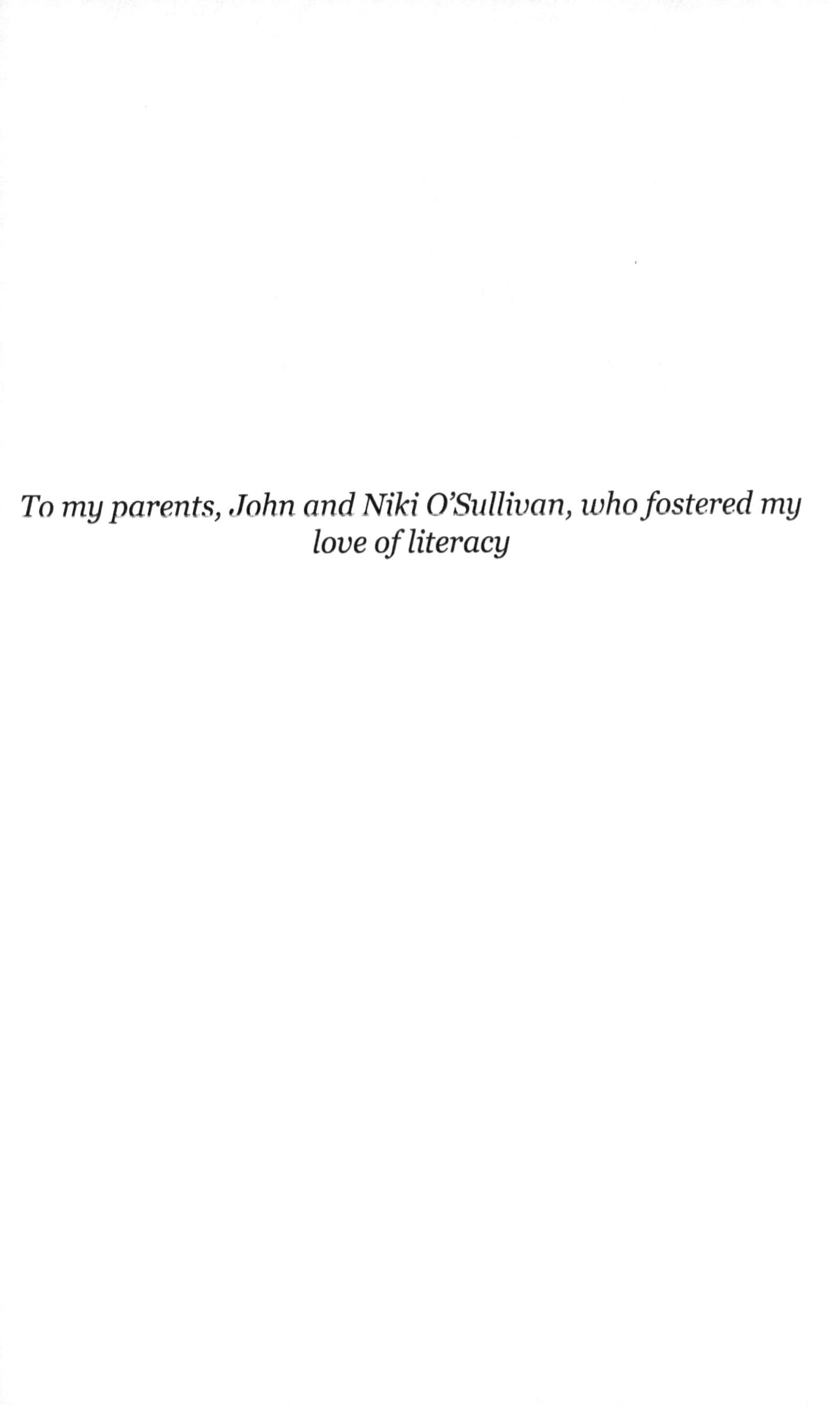

*To my parents, John and Niki O'Sullivan, who fostered my
love of literacy*

PROLOGUE

The water—gleaming, shiny, and black in the faint moonlight—chills her skin despite the warm, humid air. Her toes push further into the sediment, squishing past weeds and over a sharp rock or piece of glass, sending a spasm of pain up her right leg.

I wonder if I'm bleeding? *she thinks, aware it no longer matters. She trudges forward while the lake swallows her thighs, billowing out her dress and creating the illusion of a swollen midriff. Hot tears trickle from her eyes, and a moan erupts from her lungs. She gulps air between sobs.*

These will be her last breaths.

She doesn't struggle; resistance is futile. When the water rises past her nose, she squeezes her eyes closed, as if for protection. She holds her breath until she can't any longer, assaulted by the burn, and draws in the cold, murky water. Thrashing, she tries to push up those few inches to the surface, to the air, to life.

Regret floods her consciousness when the water invades her lungs.

How could I let this happen? she wonders, picturing the stern but loving face of her father, the gentle smile of her mother, the mischievous grin of her little cousin missing his two front teeth.

And she sees his face, as well. Of course she does.

She wants to live, yet her limbs are numb, devoid of the strength survival will take.

She surrenders to the nothingness.

Lake of Secrets

CHAPTER

ONE

I lean my forehead on the smooth, cool glass of the window, looking out at my millionth tree. "I can't believe you're seriously doing this to me. I think this is a form of child abuse," I mutter.

"Hush," Mom replies, squinting at the GPS display screen. "Do I turn here? I can't tell if Richard means this street or if it's up there."

Richard is the name my parents use for the disembodied voice of the GPS, like he's a tiny British man living in our car to guide us around.

"Not that I should tell you, but turn here." For all her education and accomplishments, my mom is hopeless at directions. "What are you even going to do without me for the whole summer, Mom? You know you need me. You can't even read the GPS right."

"I'll be fine." She smiles through my petty criticism and turns onto a narrow road flanked by cornfields. "I managed years without it, just like you'll manage to survive this summer living a simpler life. And Aunt Evelyn could really use your help around her place. You know, she's a little old lady, all alone."

"I don't see *you* volunteering for the job of nursing home assistant," I say, the words bitter in my mouth.

Mom's eyebrows, which don't quite match her dyed auburn hair, knit together. She purses her lips as if to respond to my gibe. "Callie, I want you to make the most out of this situation and your time with Aunt Evelyn."

I can't help but question what she *really* wants to say to me, what flutters beneath her placid tone. Is she actually holding back tears, or is she just trying to make me feel bad for taunting her? Regardless, I decide to drop it.

It's too late; my bags are packed for the summer, and we're nearly there, right smack in the middle of nowhere at my great-great-aunt's house in rural Pennsylvania.

About half an hour passes at a mind-numbingly slow pace. I teeter between wanting an end to this tedious ride and clinging to the security of my mother's car despite everything.

We pull up the long, unpaved driveway in the sparsely populated cul-de-sac. The tires crunch over the gravel. I have only been here twice before, when I was much younger. What once seemed interesting and different now appears archaic and backward.

Though her home isn't a farm, Aunt Evelyn resides in what she calls "Mennonite country" surrounded by those who "live plainly," as she once explained to me. Our visits to Deerville were my only glimpses into the lives of people who live in a manner so different from us.

When I was a little girl, I loved watching the horses and buggies riding by, with the people in peculiar clothes peering out at me in my colorful, often sequined outfits. Now, all I can think is, *Please let my cellphone have reception out here!*

Aunt Evelyn waits for us on a front porch which boasts hanging flower baskets and a fat black cat. In spite of the peeling white paint, cracked wooden steps, and shutters barely hanging on for dear life, the building remains elegant and cheerful, just like Aunt Evelyn. In her late eighties, she is worse for wear than the last time I saw her a few years ago, hunched and scrawny. Her many decades have etched themselves onto her face in deep crevices.

Still, her fine, white hair is held in a neat bun, a string of pearls decorates her neck, and bright red lipstick graces her withered yet smiling lips. She takes care of her appearance.

Mom hefts my gigantic suitcase from the trunk, and I already regret bringing so much stuff. I glance at my surroundings and doubt I will need any of the strappy sandals or flirty sundresses I packed. Days of soccer shorts, sports bras, and oversized T-shirts are my future here.

However, when I take in the glorious sight of a decrepit, green punch buggy pulled up next to the house, I say a silent prayer of thanks to the DMV gods for the driver's license tucked into my wallet. Maybe Aunt Evelyn will let me drive it once in a while and I will be able to escape this farmland isolation.

Even though I resent Mom and Dad for taking me away from my friends and my life this summer, I am determined not to blame this sweet old lady for my problems. A genuine rush of emotion overwhelms me while I embrace Aunt Evelyn's elderly, fragile body with my young, healthy, strong one. Knowing I have grown up and she has grown older, I shouldn't be surprised I am both taller and thicker than she is now, but it is a little unsettling all the same.

"Welcome, dear." She plants a dry, papery kiss on my cheek. "I'm so happy you wanted to come." Her faded, cornflower-blue eyes light up her pale face.

I don't want to correct her with the truth: my parents are forcing me to stay here.

What has Mom told her? After all, there is no major issue. I didn't get pregnant, get expelled, or start a high school drug cartel or anything. In fact, I didn't even get in trouble with my parents, which makes this whole thing completely ridiculous. Basically, they thought I was too caught up in shopping and social media and what not—normal teenage stuff—and they wanted me to experience a simpler, more nature-filled life with a family member who could use the company.

It is not supposed to be a punishment, but the fact they are mandating me to spend almost my whole summer vacation between junior and senior year away from home and friends makes it feel like a prison sentence.

Mom is jabbering away about the gorgeous sky—it's blue, like back home—plentiful trees—who cares—and fresh scents—smells like cow poop to me, gross—while we make our way into Aunt Evelyn's house. The cat winds itself through my legs, its fluffy tail tickling my bare calves, and I am grateful for this small comfort. We have a strict no-cats policy at home because of my little sister's allergies.

"That's Luna. She used to be a stray," Aunt Evelyn explains.

We shuffle into a living room crowded with furniture and knick-knacks, mostly cat figurines. She stoops to grab her pet, cuddling Luna close against her thin chest.

"She's a wonderful companion. I was so lonely after my Marigold died." She points a finger toward the wall, where an orange, equally rotund cat lounges in a framed photograph.

This stirs up a vivid memory from my childhood: lying out back under Aunt Evelyn's weeping willow tree with Marigold on my lap, a gentle breeze to alleviate the heat, and a good book to read. I couldn't have felt more peaceful or content. Maybe I will be able to capture some of that again while I am here.

Aunt Evelyn sits down on a worn sofa and gestures for us to do so as well. I push aside a throw pillow bearing the embroidered message "No outfit is complete without cat hair" and sink into an easy chair. Framed photographs adorn almost every inch of space over the faded floral wallpaper, surrounding Marigold. I recognize myself in a tutu around age three, along with dozens of pictures of Mom, my uncle, and two or three generations of cousins.

"I take comfort in my pictures," Aunt Evelyn says, noticing my gaze. "Even though many of my loved ones are long gone, at least I feel close to them. Look, Grace, there's your grandmother and me and one of her friends, as girls. Callie, your great-grandmother. I must've been about seven there, which would make her seventeen."

In black and white from within the gilt frame, three girls smile in matching white shirts and conservative plaid skirts. Aunt Evelyn and Great-Grandma, small-boned and blond, look almost like the same person at different ages, with the friend a sturdier, darker centerpiece.

I try to merge this childish, vibrant image of Aunt Evelyn with the aged one sitting in front of me and come up with nothing. My great-grandmother near the end was shriveled and ravaged with cancer, helpless in her hospital bed. Time is cruel.

Mom and Aunt Evelyn spend a few minutes chatting about various family members and reminiscing about Mom's own childhood visits. But I sense visiting hours are up. I can read my mother pretty well most of the time, and she seems ready to leave, anxious to ditch me.

Sure enough, Mom peels herself from the couch and gathers her purse and sunglasses. "Aunt Evelyn, thank you for hosting Callie. It means so much to Oscar and me that you're giving her the opportunity to do more with her summer."

Mom's tone is genuine, and I feel validated that she hasn't led Aunt Evelyn to believe I am a juvenile delinquent or something. Still, how will I be doing *more* with my summer? It doesn't look like I will be doing much of anything—mowing the lawn, maybe, or helping weed the garden. If Mom was so desperate for me to do something, I could have gotten a job, done community service, or taken a summer class as part of a pre-college program. Sometimes, I just don't get that lady.

"I have to leave, I'm afraid. Oscar's home with Mia right now, but he'll have to go back to the office, and I need to take her to swim practice," Mom continues.

My jealousy flares at the mention of my little sister's normal summer routine. Her life will go on without a hitch, while I am stuck out here in the boonies.

I must have made a face because Mom takes a hold of my shoulders and hugs me. She is not a hugger, preferring to show her affection through other ways, such as special treats or gifts.

"Callie, I love you and will miss you, and so will your dad and sister. But I think you'll enjoy your time here in Deerville. I did, and I want you to have the same experience."

I maintain an icy glare for about two seconds until tears glimmer in her eyes. Even though I am upset, I can't *not* say goodbye to my mom, and I don't want to appear to be a petulant teenager in front of innocent Aunt Evelyn. I hug her back, needing to clear my throat a bit before murmuring, "I love you too, and I'll *miss* you"—this last part to drive home the point that she is abandoning me.

I will miss her, though. Yes, I am mad that she is doing this to me, but I have never been away from my parents for more than a few days before, let alone a whole summer.

Aunt Evelyn and I stand on the porch, watching Mom drive away in her little gold Honda. The weight of the vast stretch of days settles upon me.

Aunt Evelyn's bony fingers land on my wrist, faint and cool to the touch. Although I am trying to be on my best behavior and not let her know how oppressive this visit feels to me, I think she must understand on some level. Maybe she remembers being that little girl in the picture, forced to be at the beck and call of the grownups.

"How about some lunch?" she asks, even though it is only about 10:30 in the morning.

I nod in acquiescence while my mother's car disappears beyond the bend, back to civilization.

21

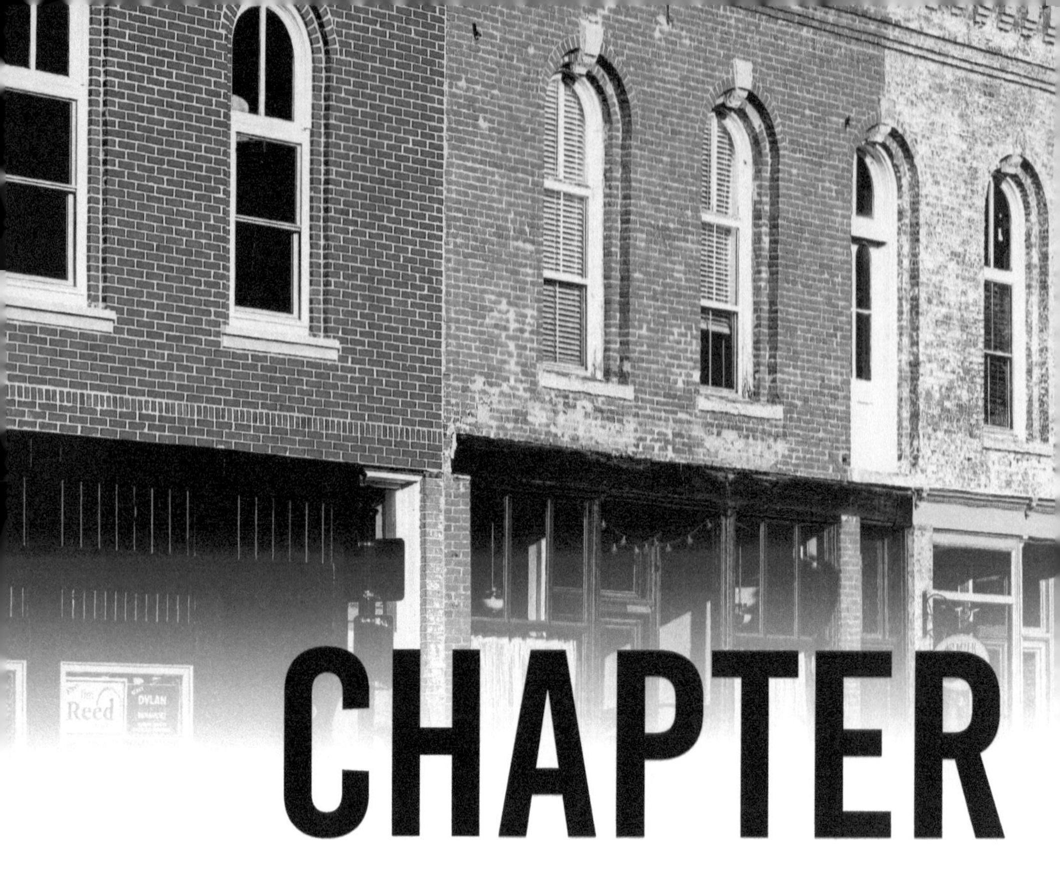

CHAPTER

TWO

The first few days pass by in a slow and painful haze. I fall into Aunt Evelyn's routine, which she is quick to explain.

She starts each morning with some stretches and a brief walk around the cul-de-sac. Sundays are for doing laundry. Mondays are light cleaning days. Tuesdays are reserved for weeding and gardening, although she has a "nice young man" to mow the lawn. Wednesdays are set aside to "just relax" by doing crossword puzzles and watching television. Appointments usually happen on Thursdays. Friday mornings are for going out to breakfast, sometimes with friends—a "dwindling number," she tells me—followed by grocery shopping and a trip to the gas station to replenish the tiny amount of fuel she uses. Saturday is her time off.

Somewhere between a complicated March Madness tournament bracket and complete monotony, her schedule seldom varies.

"It's important for little old ladies like me to have our routines." After writing it all out for me in a somewhat shaky scrawl on a piece of *Garfield* paper, she secures it onto the fridge with a souvenir magnet from Niagara Falls. "It keeps me sane."

I nod. Twenty-four hours might feel interminable to her. Does she see her life as a long expanse of time she needs to fill up with small tasks?

Back home, each day zooms by in a blur: I wake up at 5:30, get ready, go to school, play sports or attend other extra-curricular activities, come home and do homework for a few hours, have maybe half an hour to watch TV or mess around on my phone, go to bed, and do it all again. Whereas my normal schedule makes my head spin at times, it is hard to imagine Aunt Evelyn's being fulfilling to me. I don't tell her this, wanting to spare her feelings.

She is also like clockwork when it comes to meals. Aunt Evelyn rises and bathes at 6:00 and likes some time to sit on the porch with her decaf coffee before pouring a bowl of cereal or toasting some raisin bread promptly at 7:00. Lunch is at 10:30, and dinner is at 4:30. We fix easy-to-prepare and not-so-tasty meals, like frozen pizza or the ever-popular hot dog microwaved in a paper towel and served on a defrosted bun.

"If I'm feeling wild, I like to drive into town to get a sandwich from the Subway or the Burger King," Aunt Evelyn tells me, clarifying her food consumption practices.

After the first few days of this diet, I make a mental note to add some fruit and greens into the cart during the next shopping trip, which I look forward to in a way never matched by my former tedium at the supermarket, when forced to accompany Mom or Dad.

The truth is, I don't know Aunt Evelyn very well. I haven't visited since I was ten. My desire to be on my best behavior overpowers my ability to act like myself, so I am walking on eggshells while I navigate through my new domestic arrangement.

Not that I should be surprised, but there is no Wi-Fi. My internet use is limited to my phone, which usually can't get a signal, and it is slow when it comes, so web surfing is more like web rippling. When I am lucky, I can at least send or receive texts, but this gets old fast when I hardly hear back from anyone. It is disappointing, but I guess it is out of sight, out of mind, and all my friends are off enjoying their regular lives.

Desperate for outside contact, I even text my chem lab partner—a goofy but nice guy—but we have nothing more to talk about than how we did on our finals and if either of us is doing anything interesting over the summer.

My bedroom is the same as on my childhood visits—modest-sized, with a four-poster bed and rose-patterned wallpaper. I felt like a princess when sleeping here as a kid and the trip was an adventure, a break in routine, rather than the torture it feels like now. All I notice is the stuffiness of the room, how it seems like a chamber of claustrophobia.

Even with this space of my own, I try to spend a good amount of time with Aunt Evelyn, not wanting to be an ungrateful houseguest. When not helping her with her chores, I sit in the living room in the squishy chair, half read a yellowing, dog-eared copy of *Anna Karenina* I found in my room, and half watch whatever old show appears on the television—the most modern object in the house.

She doesn't subscribe to Netflix, Hulu, or Max, but she has all these old-timey stations I have never heard of. With my divided attention, I can barely keep straight all the Russian nicknames or cowboys' names, so lackadaisical is my attention. I follow both and neither.

Perhaps being elderly makes people cold. Aunt Evelyn never seems to mind the lack of air conditioning, while I sit in the stifling house with sweat streaming from my pores. Guilt nags at me when Aunt Evelyn puts a sweater on to come into a room where I have opened a window and turned on the ceiling fan, but I can't breathe in the muggy June heat.

I have done the Jumble, the Cryptoquip, and the crossword puzzle every day. They take hours and have given me a small but important sense of accomplishment. By the third day of my servitude as Aunt Evelyn's shadow—after cleaning, gardening, lots of *Bonanza* and *The Rifleman*, and plenty of chatting about the various behaviors of the cat—Aunt Evelyn meets my gaze with knowing eyes over our microwaved lunch.

"Callie, you've been so sweet, but I don't need you to pretend to be a little old lady too. I know my life isn't very exciting." She waves a wrinkled hand in the air when I start to protest, always mindful of her feelings. "Honey, I had my excitement...and plenty of it. Oh, if walls could talk..."

I look around the walls crammed with dead cats and people, aware of the age and unknown history of this house. An eerie chill creeps up my spine. *Um, I hope not.* I am still getting used to the mysterious sounds I hear in the deep quiet of the night, telling myself it is just the creaking of the house or the midnight escapades of Luna.

My great-great-aunt reads my discomfort. "I've been on my own for most of my life. I'm a spinster—an old maid, as you know. Now a really old maid." She laughs at her little joke. "It's just been me ever since my mama and daddy died. Your great-grandma left long before that. She couldn't wait to get away from here, so she married your great-grandpa practically right out of high school, and the two of them moved upstate. I stayed here. Even after I finally grew up and could leave, I never did." She gestures about herself, seemingly dismissing her surroundings, her life, as bereft of meaning.

Aunt Evelyn pauses. Is there any weight to her words? A distant resentment of sibling rivalry? I take a gulp of my Diet Coke and swallow loudly, waiting for her to come back from wherever she is, from those years from which we are so far removed today.

Aunt Evelyn shakes her head as if to banish ghosts of the past. "What I'm saying, dear, is that you don't need to worry about me. I know my limits. I have my routine, and I 'live deliberately,' as Mr. Thoreau would say. Mine is a quiet life I've carved out for myself, and you are welcome to join me, but you won't hurt this old biddy's feelings if you want to get away and take the bug out for a spin in town. Your mother told me that you have your license and that you're a safe, experienced driver."

Her eyes twinkle with this last bit, which may have been a tiny exaggeration on my mother's part, but a rush of gratitude fills my heart.

"You'd let me drive the car? Really?" I ask, as if the rusty hunk of metal is a magic chariot to deliver me from my boredom into the Olympus of the outside world.

She giggles, a reedy, girlish sound that lightens the mood. "Callie, I love you, but I haven't had a long-term guest since your mother was your age. I think we both need some alone time, and I know you won't be saddened to miss a few episodes of *Bonanza*."

I almost feel hurt, realizing my hours of attentiveness haven't been the blessing to Aunt Evelyn I assumed they would be. Except for our ages and ideas of what constitutes a good time, maybe Aunt Evelyn and I aren't all that different.

After running a brush through my thick, dark hair and putting on a sleeveless top and cute jeans shorts, which are a tiny bit tight after three days of microwaved food and lethargy, I am ready to get out of the house. I glance in the full-length mirror in my room and admire my transformation.

In the last few days, I have worn nothing but baggy T-shirts and athletic shorts. I even dab a little mascara on my lashes and add a bit of lip gloss but skip the eyeliner, not wanting to seem like I am trying too hard for such a simple outing. After all, I have very few memories of the town of Deerville, and I don't want to feel silly if my only option is to hang out near the local hardware store or something equally pathetic.

Aunt Evelyn has no idea what kind of places in town will interest someone my age. I suppress a chuckle when she tells me she thinks the ice cream parlor she and her friends went to at my age was closed. Although the image of Aunt Evelyn and her friends hanging out there, flirting with boys while scandalously flashing their ankles and Oxford shoes under long dresses, sharing ice cream sodas or whatever they used to eat and drink, is delightful and intriguing.

When I tell her I am just looking to get a feel for the town, she is happy to explain how to get to Main Street.

I open the creaky door and climb inside the VW bug. After writing down some simple directions she then insists that I tape onto the dashboard, despite my protestations that I can use my Maps app—well, if I can get a signal—Aunt Evelyn allows me to drive into town by myself. Nearly itching with anticipation for something, anything, other than what I have been doing the past few days, I back out of the long driveway and head to town.

With the windows rolled down, I drive past the Mennonite farms, sighing in happiness at my outing, delighting in the crisp, blue sky and fluffy marshmallow clouds. Everything even smells better than it did on the way here. I ignore the cow dung and focus on the freshness of the air instead. Not even the broken radio dampens my spirits. I start a Spotify playlist on my iPhone.

The summer doesn't seem so bleak after all.

CHAPTER

THREE

When I reach Main Street, I crawl down the road until a dusty-looking bookstore catches my eye, then pull into the mostly vacant parking lot. While my only agenda, really, is to get out of the house, I will happily trade in the long-winded descriptions of Levin's farming processes in *Anna Karenina* for just about anything else to read. I turn off the car and hand-roll the windows up. Aunt Evelyn's squishy, hairy, anemone-looking keychain is hard to cram into my purse while I head to the front of the store.

A fluorescent welcome sign blares in the dim window of Burke's Books, but the cold eyes of the balding man at the cash register give off no such feeling. I meet his gaze and look away, feeling ashamed without quite understanding why. Self-conscious, I tug at my shorts, wishing them to be an inch or two longer, even though I can wear them to school without getting such judgmental looks from any teacher or administrator.

Since I am the only person in the whole place, one would think the guy would try to be a little less hostile.

Burke's Books is no Barnes & Noble. Instead of the colorful, glossy displays and rows of brightly lit books organized and classified by genre and author, most of these appear used. They are all stacked in a haphazard way, like someone scooped the whole lot of them from on top of the dead, flat cats in some hoarder's basement and shoved them onto shelves. Visible dust motes sparkle in a shaft of light coming through the window, and I fight my urge to sneeze.

In case the creepy guy at the counter is watching me, I pull a random volume off a shelf and inspect the cover: *Personal Financial Planning*. Um, no. My life is boring enough right now.

I get excited when I spot a couple of novels by Dennis Lehane which don't seem to be in bad condition, but I have already read them.

After several minutes of fruitless searching, I decide to make the clerk earn his money. "Excuse me," I whisper, like I am in a library full of studiers rather than a store with no other customers.

Nothing. He seems to be reading a newspaper.

"Excuse me," I say again, a little louder this time.

"Yes," he finally replies, not exactly falling over himself to provide me with assistance. He peers at me over the top of his half-moon glasses.

Now I am the one taking my time, unsure what I want to ask. "Do you have any bestsellers?" I am annoyed with myself for my timidity, as well as what must come across as the dismissal of hundreds of years of mind-altering literature in exchange for anything modern.

"Depends on what year you want. This may not meet your standards if you want a fancy, 'big business' type of bookstore." He gestures around the tiny shop.

"I don't care." Great, now I am really showing my intelligence. "I just want something interesting, you know?"

He takes his sweet time, lifts the partition in the counter, and strolls over to me, hands in the pockets of his shapeless khaki pants. "I suppose you want something like that *Hunger Games* or *Twilight* nonsense that you kids like, huh?" he says, more than a decade behind the times when it comes to popular teen fiction. He comes closer, and I can tell he is a smoker, both from his yellow teeth and the stale odor emanating from his body. "You don't look like you're from around here."

I step back, not used to twenty questions when I go to the

bookstore—or any store, for that matter—at my mall back home. "No. I'm visiting my aunt. Uh, Evelyn Reynolds." My mind flashes to kindergarten and the "stranger danger" mantra we learned.

Have I already said too much? Do I just run out of the store?

But something surprising happens. That cranky mouth turns up at the ends, and a moment later, I realize he is smiling. In fact, everything about his body language is different.

"Ms. Reynolds? Out in the country? That's your aunt?" He is almost glowing.

"Yes." A pregnant pause passes while I attempt to contort my own grimace into something resembling a friendly expression. "My great-great-aunt, actually. My great-grandmother's sister."

"She was my teacher back in the seventh grade. Science class, it was."

He waits for me to fill the silence, but I can't fathom what he wants me to say. I didn't even know Aunt Evelyn was a teacher—a fact that makes me feel guilty. Have I asked her about her life at all, or did we always just make small talk? It is hard for me to imagine her in any sort of role apart from that of an ancient lady filling her days with old television shows and her "routine."

He continues, extending his hand, which I shake. "Bruce Burke. That's me on the sign." The lord of the manor. He raises his hand in a flourish toward the crooked lettering on the storefront.

"Nice to meet you," I say, marveling at his new attitude. Within the lapse of a minute, he has metamorphosed from Grumpy the dwarf to Happy, all the while defying stereotypes of every other bookseller I have ever met. "Uh, I'm Callie."

"Great to meet you! We don't get many city folk here." To emphasize his point, he points outside, where the sole action consists of a wide, elderly gentleman waddling down the sidewalk of Main Street.

After all those Westerns I have been watching, I half expect a tumble weed to appear as a manifestation of the sheer stillness, something I never see back home. Cagney might not be a bustling metropolis, but it is like New York City compared to Deerville.

Mr. Burke flicks his eyes back and forth, as if to check that no one else is watching, and leans in. "People 'round here can get fussy over strangers. Best to tell them about your familial connections."

Yes. All the cool kids will like me once they find out I am

spending the summer with an elderly relative.

Ten or so minutes later, I exit the store with a smiley-faced plastic bag full of books: Stephen King, Toni Morrison, Ken Follett, Amy Tan, Carol Goodman, even an ancient-looking copy of *The Scarlet Letter*—nothing recent, but well-loved literature which may help me pass the days.

Although Mr. Burke balked when I presented my debit card, saying he didn't have any of "those fancy doo-dads" to take my order, the price was so cheap that I actually had enough cash to pay for it. That is one advantage of a used bookstore. I can buy everything for the price of what one new book would cost me.

I make a mental note to find an ATM, in case other stores in town are also disinclined to plastic. One bonus of my parents' guilt at sending me here: they deposited a few hundred dollars into my bank account for "incidentals" before I left.

A glance at my phone indicates only about thirty minutes have passed. I am accustomed to a much tighter schedule at home, so I don't often have five minutes to relax, but now the weight of time bears down on me. There is nothing to do but explore my surroundings a little more.

I am certainly not excited about most of the shops on Main Street. Although it is nice to see some mom-and-pop operations—a far cry from the blocks of nothing but chain businesses back home—Joe's Auto Parts and Ned's Hardware are of absolutely zero interest to me.

Not wanting to go back to Aunt Evelyn's just yet, I look around for a Starbucks and settle on Nan's Coffee Shop and Bakery. One thing I can say for Deerville: the small business owners are all transparent about what they are selling.

After the depressing dustiness of Burke's Books and the other equally grungy storefronts, I am pleasantly surprised by the colorful cheeriness of the coffee cup-shaped sign hanging over Nan's. It is either a relic from the 1950s or modeled to appear like it, shiny and clean, with a glistening black and white checkerboard floor. I set my bag of books down at a booth.

Unlike the desolation of Burke's and Main Street in general, Nan's has about a dozen customers ranging from a mom with three little boys to an old couple. A guy and girl about my age are sharing an ice cream sundae, which must be what constitutes a date for teenagers in Deerville. It is kind of sweet and innocent, and I can't help but wonder what their lives are like, if kids here are plagued with all the same issues I see back home.

Does the high school have drug busts and arrests, like mine does? Do they have the same kinds of problems with the vicious cycle of teenage pregnancy? I consider introducing myself to the couple and asking those questions, but only for half a second. After all, I don't want to be viewed as a freak or, even worse, as someone making fun of their small-town lives.

Instead of acting like a total creeper and giving those strangers a story to regale their friends with, I walk up to the counter. The rows of pastries catch my eyes first, but what I spot next looks even better.

It is something I haven't seen since I left Cagney.

A hot guy.

After days with no one to look at but Aunt Evelyn, he is a sight for sore eyes. He is about my age and tall, with tan skin, sandy-colored hair, and bright blue eyes. *Piercing* blue eyes. He throws me off when he speaks to me.

"Hi. Ready to order?" he asks.

I say nothing for too long, paranoid he noticed me checking him out. "Uh, a cappuccino? With skim milk? And a cookie?" I don't know why I am giving my order in questions. Embarrassed, I try to tamp down the heat rising to my face, but the blush sneaks up on me all the same.

"Okay. What size? And what kind of cookie?" he asks, patient enough.

I obviously haven't quite made the same impression on him that he made on me.

Five minutes later, I am safely ensconced in my booth with my cappuccino and giant white chocolate macadamia nut cookie, having survived the mortification of ordering from the Greek god behind the counter.

Just my luck: creepy old Mr. Burke gave me an earful and wanted to know all about me in return, but Hot Coffee Guy has no interest in meeting an exotic stranger from out of town. Leila, my best friend back home, wouldn't have stammered her order and probably would have walked away with his phone number. Even better, he might have asked for hers.

Oh, well. I have never been good at flirting. Still, I chastise myself not for that, but for judging this guy on looks alone. For all I know, he might beat up kittens and babies for fun. And it is not like I want to be the kind of girl who picks up guys in coffee shops anyway.

I get over my rejection, or whatever it was, and settle back in the comfortable booth, contemplating my happiness: coffee, cookie, books. These are a few of my favorite things, and I have all of them. I reach into my bag and grab the book on top: *The Scarlet Letter*.

It isn't one I know much about, just that it is something about an adulteress. Mrs. Hunter, my favorite teacher last year, recommended it, warning me to start at Chapter 1, skipping the introduction. This seemed like an illogical instruction from someone who loves literature as much as she does, but I trust her judgment and am willing to take her advice.

Despite my less-than-quiet environment, with various chit chat, loud coffee machine noises, a crying toddler, and some old Elvis song playing on a retro jukebox in the corner, I am pretty good at blocking out my surroundings and sinking my teeth into a good book. But I haven't even made it through half my coffee or Hester's public shaming on the scaffold when something flutters out of the pages, past the table, and all the way to the checkerboard floor, distracting me.

It is a newspaper clipping—an aged, yellowing one. Curious, I pick it up, figuring it is someone's bookmark.

The headline compels me to leave Hester to the goodwives and keep reading.

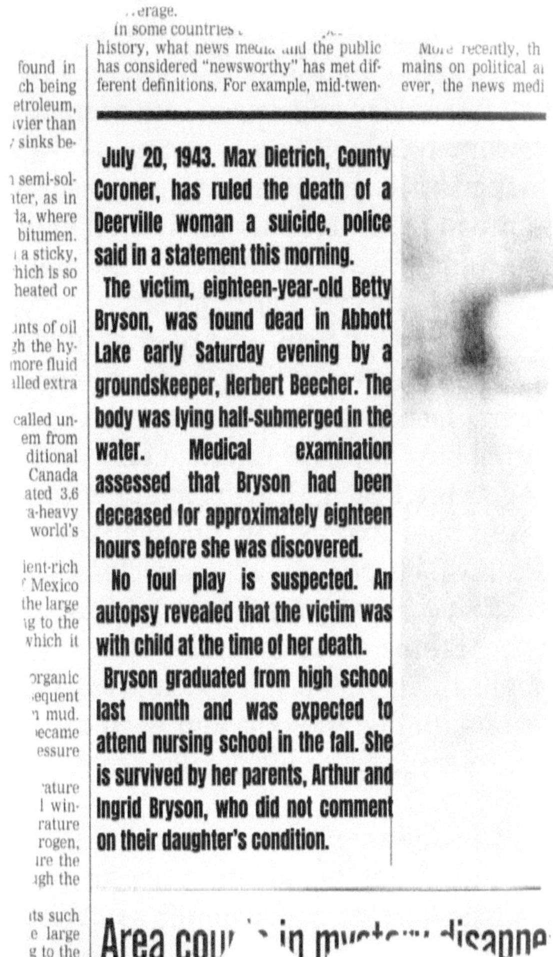

July 20, 1943. Max Dietrich, County Coroner, has ruled the death of a Deerville woman a suicide, police said in a statement this morning.

The victim, eighteen-year-old Betty Bryson, was found dead in Abbott Lake early Saturday evening by a groundskeeper, Herbert Beecher. The body was lying half-submerged in the water. Medical examination assessed that Bryson had been deceased for approximately eighteen hours before she was discovered.

No foul play is suspected. An autopsy revealed that the victim was with child at the time of her death.

Bryson graduated from high school last month and was expected to attend nursing school in the fall. She is survived by her parents, Arthur and Ingrid Bryson, who did not comment on their daughter's condition.

And that's it? No picture of the victim, no reason why foul play wasn't suspected? Did they assume she killed herself because she was pregnant?

A chill runs through me. This girl was barely older than I am now, yet her whole life was dismissed in a few brief paragraphs.

Every teenager imagines life after high school. Our futures might not be as rosy as we hope, but we still want those futures. Why would she have enrolled in nursing school if she was just going to kill herself? And who kills herself by drowning? What a depressing way to go.

I think back to last summer with my parents and Mia. We vacationed in Cabo San Lucas in Mexico. Although the beaches are beautiful there, some of the waves are truly wicked, so the hotels warn vacationers not to go in the water. I listened to the advice but was careless when walking too close to the water's edge.

A wave lapped my ankles and seized one of my favorite Adidas slides right out of my hands. When I ventured into the water just past my knees to reclaim it, the waves captured me as well, dragging me out to sea. Though the water was shallow enough that I should have been able to stand, I was smashed back down by one crashing wave after another with my every attempt.

I couldn't scream, cry for help, or breathe, inhaling salt water through my mouth and nose every time I tried. Metallic blood coated my tongue after my face was slammed repeatedly into the ocean floor. I kept fighting but thought I might actually lose the battle.

When I looked at the beach, praying silently for help, I noticed my mother—a horrified expression on her face—start running toward the water. I wondered if my last conscious sight would be of her encountering a similar fate. Mother to join daughter in death.

I shudder at the trauma of the memory.

For me, though, there was a happy ending. A local man saw what was happening, pulled me out, and even rescued my stupid shoe. After being released from his strong arms, I collapsed onto the beach.

My parents and passersby gathered around me while I spluttered and coughed out water, snot, blood, and tears all over the sand. My mom discreetly helped me twist my swimming suit back into position and checked my wounds. Just scrapings, she told me, and I had bitten my lip, drawing blood. Physically, I was fine.

My parents tried to give my rescuer money, but he refused. A true hero, he walked off to the other side of the beach. Satisfied I was okay, the crowd which had gathered dispersed and forgot my near drowning.

It wasn't quite so easy for me. Although I can't say I was haunted by it for weeks to come, I spent the rest of the day wrapped in a towel, picking sand out of my hair, crying on and off, terrified of what could have happened. The thought of standing on the precipice of death at sixteen was awful.

Why had this Betty wanted to die in this way? Why didn't her parents demand more answers?

I run my fingers through my hair. My ears catch the melody

playing on the jukebox. It is an old-fashioned song, one I have never heard before. Something about a moonlight cocktail? I try to read a little more but am too distracted. As much as I am intrigued by how Hester stands tall and ladylike in the face of all the judgment upon her, I can't shake the thought of Betty Bryson and her unborn child, their lives extinguished in a watery grave.

I drain my cappuccino, stick the newspaper clipping back into my book to mark my place, grab my bag, and leave Nan's without another glance at the handsome guy behind the counter.

Maybe piercing blue eyes are what got poor Betty into trouble.

CHAPTER

FOUR

I drive back to Aunt Evelyn's, figuring I have had enough action for one day. Now I sound like her, arranging my days around non-events like driving to town, buying books, and grabbing coffee. I am sure I will get used to the time and solitude, luxuries which don't exist for me at home, but so far, too much time has felt as troublesome as not enough.

Aunt Evelyn asks me about my outing, so I deliver Mr. Burke's cheerful salutations and let her recount his antics in her classroom long ago. I also tell her about stopping at Nan's and how cute I think it is.

"Nan's has been around for ages," she says. "Believe it or not, your great-grandmother and I used to go there as girls. It wasn't so modern-looking back then."

I suppress a smirk. Aunt Evelyn is so old that retro takes on a whole new meaning with her.

"Oh, those were good old days back then." Her eyes cloud over in that familiar way while she walks down memory lane, to a time when she was young and beautiful, a era when her friends and loved ones were plentiful rather than dead and buried in the ground. "Some people think we romanticize our youth. Maybe so. I remember the ugliness too. But when I was a young girl, living here with my parents and sister, life was simple."

She frowns, with more creases lining her wrinkled face, and fingers the pearls of her necklace.

"Even after America was dragged into the war, there was a certain excitement in the air. Men died for their country, and we girls and women at home did what we could to support their efforts. People had honor and dignity."

I can't help but wonder what she is suppressing. Her life seems simple to me. She doesn't appear to have worries. What am I missing? I would like to ask, but I am always apprehensive about upsetting her, and I don't want to be impolite.

But I should know more about her, my living, breathing insight into history, so I try to get her back to a happy place. "Tell me more, Aunt Evelyn. I'd love to hear more about you and Great-Grandma."

She looks almost through me for a moment, shaking herself back from whatever glimpse into the past she is seeing. A slight smile returns to her lips.

"Another time, dear. Perry Mason is about to come on the television."

I have heard that you dream more when you don't watch a lot of TV. Perhaps my half watching of all those old shows doesn't really count.

While sleeping, my mind spins visions of Hester's simple jail cell and a dead girl in a lake. She is face down in the water with her shoeless, mud-streaked legs poking out on the grass. Her hair spreads out in a dark, limp fan around her head.

Crafted by Hawthorne and my own overactive imagination, a mash-up of decades and characters collides, and I wake up feeling anxious. In my dream, I touched her. I rolled her around to look at her face, only for my own dead eyes to stare back at me. And then she/I opened her/my mouth and said...

I can't remember, but the voice was distant, like it wasn't even coming from the corpse's mouth, but somewhere deeper and farther away.

In the suffocating room, my skin has broken out in goosebumps, my pulse racing. I press the home button on my iPhone and see the numbers 12:17.

Of course it is. It is during the witching hour.

I don't often have scary dreams, especially when I haven't been watching or reading something of that nature. And I was only reading Hawthorne, not the Stephen King novel I purchased. Feeling childish and silly, I take a deep breath, trying to calm myself.

I imagine a picture of tranquility to help me get back to sleep: palm trees, a warm sun, hot sand under my body...This usually works for me, but this peaceful scene just brings me back to the violence of my near drowning last year and the deceased girl.

I switch to counting sheep instead and eventually nod off again.

Somehow, I sleep past eight, which must seem absolutely scandalous to Aunt Evelyn. After getting up to brush my teeth, I catch my reflection. My hair, pulled up into a bun, looks like a rat's nest on top of my head. Although I slept late, dark bags pool beneath my bloodshot eyes.

My eyes.

The dream rushes back, and I suppress a shudder. My own vacant eyes in the dead girl's body.

I walk back into my bedroom, gingerly take the crumbling clipping from *The Scarlet Letter*, and consider throwing it away, but I don't. It seems wrong somehow. Betty died, and someone cared enough to save the clipping.

Despite its creepy connotation, I tuck it back into the book to mark my place, preserving Betty's existence.

Restless, I decide to go for a quick run. With all these thoughts, I can't just sit around watching TV this morning. I change quickly and grab my MP3 player and Garmin watch, yell a quick explanation to Aunt Evelyn, and head out the door.

It is a humid day, as usual, but it is only in the high 70s, and I already feel great about getting my blood pumping through my veins. After that dream, I need to do something life-affirming. I breathe in and out, falling into a steady pace, confident I won't get lost.

It is so different from running at home, where I am constantly stopping for cars before crossing the street. I feel alone but in a fantastic way. The fields ripple—green grass dappled with wildflowers under a broad expanse of blue sky. The surface of a lake glimmers in the sunlight, and a morning mist hovers over it like cotton. I check my watch—a castoff from my dad, who used to run but can't since he messed up his knee.

Two miles in, I am feeling wonderful.

My radio goes all scratchy.

The MP3 player was also my dad's. My music is all on my phone, but I don't like running with it since it is too big and throws off my balance. I deleted my dad's middle-aged-man music but never got around to adding my own, so I always listen to the radio. Now, though, I just have static.

Sweat drips down my face. I stop running and try to switch stations.

Great. Nothing is coming in.

Finally, I hit something clear—some oldies station. Well, it is better than nothing.

My limbs pump once again, and I concentrate on the lyrics.

Mix in a couple of dreamers and there you are:
Lovers hail the Moonlight Cocktail.

Of course. I just heard it at Nan's yesterday. Weird. Not exactly good running music, but it is better than static or the sound of my own breathing, which is especially labored since I haven't run in a while. It is a pretty song, actually, and I enjoy it until I trip on something and fall hard on my hands and knees, scraping my flesh on the rough road.

"Dammit," I mutter aloud.

With no one to witness my pain and embarrassment, except the regal red-winged blackbirds flying overhead, I scoot over onto the grass under a massive beech tree to keep myself shaded. I go to press pause on my running watch, which I didn't wreck in my klutziness, not wanting to mess up the counter of my pace with this annoying interlude. But the watch has stopped on its own. The numbers blink.

Did I lose satellite reception? Oh well. It isn't like I am training for a marathon or anything, so I guess it doesn't really matter what my pace is.

I glance behind me to find what I tripped on, but there is nothing, not uneven pavement or a root burrowing through the road. It must have been my own stupid feet.

My palms and knees sting, so I inspect my road rash. The skin is split and torn, bleeding slightly, with lots of little black flecks from the street already woven in. *Greeeaaat.*

I consider washing out the wound in the lake that is almost right in front of me, which appears sanitary, but I use my better judgment. Doing so could give me some crazy bacterial infection.

The lake. "Abbott Lake", the sign reads.

Abbott Lake, where the girl drowned.

This is too much for me.

I force myself to look at it—*really* look at it—and try to compare it to my dream last night. But it doesn't resemble any crime scene. In fact, it is the picture of tranquility, something one would see on a postcard advertising the serenity of rural Pennsylvania.

The clear water undulates when a couple of ducks swim through it. The soft staccato of croaking frogs echoes, hidden within the grasses. The surface mirrors the glorious sun. Pussy willows and Queen Anne's lace add to the wild but beautiful splendor.

Still, all I can think is that someone died here. Someone killed herself here. I would never have known, except for randomly finding that newspaper clipping yesterday.

A four-mile run will suffice. I brush myself off and head back to Aunt Evelyn's house, my skin throbbing.

A few more days into the summer and it is Aunt Evelyn who suggests I get out of the house. I can't agree more.

"What about a part-time job, dear?" she asks over our matching bowls of Cheerios. "That might add some excitement into your life and some cash into your pocketbook."

Her term *pocketbook* makes me smile. I have become accustomed to all her old lady-isms. "Sure. Do you think they're hiring in town?"

"Oh, sweetie, I'm sure someone's hiring. A lot of the children your age don't bother trying to work. They're content to let their parents pay for everything." Her mouth hardens into a thin, straight line. "The younger generation has changed over time. When I was your age, girls were getting ready for marriage and working life. Our country had barely recovered from one war when we were thrust into another, but we were all trying to make the most of our lives.

"Today, young people want to delay growing up as long as possible. I know women almost as old as me taking care of little babies. Babies, can you imagine? My friend Martha, who used to have breakfast with me on Friday mornings, raised her granddaughter when her daughter wouldn't take care of her. Now she's raising her great-granddaughter since the granddaughter is off gallivanting around with different boyfriends! Will this one turn out any better after two failures?" Her hand clenches around her coffee mug in frustration.

I look down. Aunt Evelyn, who is normally very sweet and docile, gets cranky here and there, but I am surprised by her vehemence. Even though I am part of this "reckless" younger generation, it is not my place to contradict her.

She must sense my unease, for she is quick to explain.

"Callie, dear, not you. You're a wonderful, respectable young lady. Keep in mind, I worked with teenagers for a long time as a schoolteacher. I witnessed the shift from the days when people in my profession were revered to when we were bullied. And I've been out of the classroom for almost thirty years! When I was a girl, young ladies behaved as such. Now they run around like little trollops, walking around so scantily clad and letting boys have their way with them. It's indecent. And if girls did get into trouble, the families kept it quiet. They didn't flaunt their disgrace about like they do now. Their families sent them away when they were improper."

Does she really think it was better for a girl to be cast out and isolated from her family? I decide not to tell her about all the teen pregnancies in my school. A couple of girls have already had babies, and all I feel for them is empathy, not judgment.

In English class freshman year, there was this girl, Mikayla, who sat next to me and always tried to start up conversations. She hung out with the popular crowd in middle school, but by freshman year, she kept to herself. I found her attempts at friendship with me to be a little too clingy, so I was polite enough but kept my distance.

Then she left school one day and had a baby. Even though I had seen her every day, I didn't have a clue she was pregnant.

After people found out, they just talked trash about Mikayla, saying what a slut she was. No one mentioned a word about the guy rumored to be the father, and he went on like life was normal. Mikayla didn't come back to school sophomore year, and I couldn't blame her. I just wished I had seen her neediness for what it was: a plea for a connection. If only I had tried a little harder with her.

But I am not going to argue with my elderly relative or be condescending to her in any way. Instead, I try to direct the conversation back to the job idea. "So, do I fill out an application online?" I ask, already guessing the answer.

"In Deerville? Goodness, no!" Aunt Evelyn replies, smiling once again, distracted from the "trollops" who are nothing like the young ladies of her day. "Callie, most of our shops in town still operate on a cash system. They don't have those little credit card thingamajiggies. You go on to the stores and fill out a paper application. That's the way to do it. And wear something nice while you go to make a good impression." She glances over my sloppy, hanging-around-the-house outfit.

I hold myself back from the eye roll I would have given either of my parents for a similar comment and ask her advice. After all, she has lived in Deerville for her entire life and knows the way the town works, even if she has been a little out of touch for the past decade or three, mostly left to her own devices out in the country.

"Do you think anyone would interview me today?" I will look silly if I get all dolled up just to fill out applications.

"Well, dear, you know that old saying: 'You never get a second chance to make a first impression.' Maybe just put on a nice blouse, skirt, and pumps."

Rather than explaining to Aunt Evelyn that "pumps" are not exactly a staple of the modern teenager's wardrobe, I thank her and run upstairs to change. I am not too hopeful that I will accomplish anything with a drive into town. With how little business most of the stores have, I will be lucky if any place is hiring. But what else do I have to do?

A few minutes later, I am twirling around in front of Aunt Evelyn for inspection.

"You look beautiful and sensible," she says.

I have found a pink button-down shirt and nice-ish white capris—to hide my scabby knees—with dressy sandals. Maybe not what she had in mind, but I seem to pass her test. However, my cheap Forever 21 jewelry isn't quite up to snuff. I almost gasp when she unclasps the ever-present strand of pearls from around her neck and hands them over to me.

"My mother—your great-great grandmother—gave them to me when I was a young girl, and I've worn them ever since. I couldn't believe she would trust me with something so special, but I've taken good care of them, and I know you will too. Keep them safe for me, please," she says.

While I have always seen these around her neck, I have never had a close look. Almost perfectly round, the pearls twinkle in the soft kitchen lighting. They are unpredictably heavy, and I am surprised at the slight grittiness of their texture. Maybe that is how to tell they are the real deal.

"Are you sure?" I quickly take off my imitation gold necklace.

She nods. "Just be mindful of the clasp. Make sure it's fastened. It broke once, long ago, and I needed to get some of the pearls replaced."

I place her prized possession gingerly around my own neck. With this addition, my confidence increases. Maybe I won't get a job, but I will look good trying.

I am neither shocked nor too disappointed when my inquiries at the local DVD rental store—yes, this somehow still exists in Deerville—and hardware store are fruitless. The shopkeepers both stare at me with slack-jawed expressions when I ask if they're hiring.

It would have been cool to work in a movie store, a place I have only seen in the movies, but it is no big surprise that they are hurting for business. As for the hardware store...Well, the only way I can imagine Deerville being more boring is if I had to organize wrenches and screws all day.

Still, a job's a job, and making some cash sounds great, so I waltz down the street to the equally insipid dry cleaners.

The bell chimes my arrival into Spencer Dry Cleaning, and a slight chemical odor assaults my nostrils. Business appears somewhat promising. Not one but two customers stand in front of the counter, awaiting the drop-off or pick-up of their garments. That is two whole customers more than I saw in either of the other stores. I sit on a hard bench and try to appear patient while the guy at the counter assists them.

Even Deerville has its alternative teens. This dude's appearance screams "notice me." Though he is free of any trace of eyeliner or the requisite chipped black nail polish, his gauged ears, shaggy black hair, Metallica concert T-shirt, and skinny jeans are a far cry—howl?—from the squeaky-clean teens I have seen thus far, who look like extras in an Old Navy ad.

Emo or Goth? While I wait for my opportunity to ask for an application, I can't help but try to squeeze this dark dry cleaner into a high school hierarchy.

Finally—okay, like five minutes later—it is my turn.

"Hi," he says in a friendly tone which doesn't mesh with his eerie appearance. "Do you have your claim ticket?" He seems a little skeptical, as if he knows I am not local.

It is that familiar and weird small-town vibe where everyone knows everyone, like I have a big, shining brand on my forehead marking me as an outsider. Or maybe even a scarlet "O" embroidered on my clothing.

"I'm not picking anything up," I say. "I was wondering if you're hiring?"

He smiles and shakes his head, and I can't help but notice his white, even teeth. I try to picture him looking tough and alternative, even with the braces he most likely had.

"Contrary to that rush of business you just witnessed, we're not exactly doing great here." He waves his hand around the small shop. Although the sign outside is old, there is a fresh coat of yellow paint on the walls, and everything seems clean. "My grandpa and I are all the help we need."

"Oh," I say, unsure if I should make sympathetic noises for what seems to be hard times or if it is none of my business. "Okay, then." I settle for what I think comes off as polite but not nosy.

"You're not from around here," he continues, stating the obvious. "Deerville can be a funny place when you're not used to it."

"Yeah." Again, I am at a loss for words. The snob in me thinks I wouldn't even be talking to a guy who looks like this back in Cagney, but I have to admit, it is nice to have a conversation, however stilted, with someone who isn't an octogenarian. "I'm just here for the summer, staying with a relative."

"Evelyn Reynolds?" Reading my look of unease, he laughs. "Don't worry. I'm not a stalker. My grandpa keeps in touch with all the old people gossip. He mentioned that Ms. Reynolds had her granddaughter or someone staying with her. Or niece? I guess she never married, right?"

"Technically, great-great-niece. I'm Callie Quinn. I'm just here for the summer. I'm from Cagney."

"Welcome, Callie from Cagney," he replies in a deep, formal voice. He takes an imaginary hat from his head and bows. "I'm Brian. Brian Spencer. From Philly. I've only been living here the last few years, so trust me, I know this place takes some getting used to."

He extends his hand, and I shake it awkwardly, not accustomed to greeting people my own age like this. I guess it beats a fist bump, though, which I have never gotten into.

Brian seems nice and everything, but I am more in the market for a job than a new friend.

"So, can you think of anywhere I might be able to work? Even a few hours a week?"

"Hmm." He threads his knuckles together and bites his lip. This must be his thinking pose. "How would you feel about working with old people? I'm thinking the nursing home. They're always hiring, and we have tons of oldies here. And I guess you're used to old people already."

"Okay," I say, wondering what this will entail, but it is a start.

Brian explains how to get there, and I head back to my car, feeling relieved but maybe the tiniest bit disappointed that he didn't ask for my phone number. Not that I am into him like that or anything.

Less than an hour later, I am on my way to being employed.

Mrs. Jessica King, who serves as both human resources director and general manager of Briar Creek Manor, proclaims she is thrilled to meet me and pretty much hires me on the spot. I will be working as a dietary aide for about twenty hours per week for the rest of the summer. It seems perfect. I will make some money and have something to do, but I won't feel so monopolized that I can't do anything else. Not that there is much to do, anyway.

After the day's second handshake, a lipstick-on-teeth smile from Mrs. King, and my assurance that my mom will fax over my working permit and social security card, it is pretty much a done deal. Once the paperwork comes through, I get to start my training.

I walk out of the lobby, with its perfume of urine and cleaning products, pass the blooming lilies and roses, and smile under the warmth of the sun.

CHAPTER

FIVE

A week later, I am well-entrenched in my repetitive yet surprisingly stressful job. Depending on which position I am assigned for the shift, my tasks include serving the residents drinks, loading the industrial-strength dishwasher, calling out what food belongs on each resident's meal tray, and adding the appropriate items. While this all sounds very mundane, my coworkers are serious about their jobs and keep the pressure on. If I am too slow or make a mistake, they let me know with withering looks and clucks of disapproval.

"Don't worry. You'll get the hang of it eventually," Mary, a stout lady in her fifties, tells me when I accidentally put a piece of what we are told is steak on the tray of a resident who can only eat pureed food.

I apologize for at least the fifth time in my shift and switch the rectangle of meat for a few spoonfuls of the liquid steak—a congealing puddle of ooze tragically garnished with a sprig of parsley. Hopefully, the mysterious Mr. Matheson, the recipient of the tray, can derive some pleasure from his much tastier-looking dessert of vanilla pudding. Due to his special eating needs, he does not dine with the more able-bodied residents. Therefore, I have never seen him.

Francine, a hard-looking, bleached blond with black roots who is somehow only a year older than I am, corroborates Mary's attempts at compassion. "Don't feel bad. No one expects you to be as good as us at this job."

I am not sure if I am being bullied or excused, but I give her the benefit of the doubt. Francine's life as a self-proclaimed recovering alcoholic has followed an entirely different trajectory than my own, and I won't begrudge her the pride she takes in her work. This job is all she has for the foreseeable future, as a dropout at sixteen, but she can whip out those trays like crazy, and she doesn't make any mistakes.

It is a lesson in humility for me. I am the one getting good grades and planning to go to college in a year, but she is the one who ensures that all these residents get the right meals day after day. Mess up and give a diabetic resident a regular meal, and it could turn into a medical emergency, but that won't happen on Francine's watch.

"Callie, time to serve the drinks," Mary says.

I rush to the cart, eager to please after my screwup. In the dining room, I perform a quick scan to see which residents are already there. Randy, a pimply faced twenty-something who almost never talks, has already been around once to fill the water glasses, but it is my job to pour tea and coffee. Although everyone orders the exact same thing every time, I am still supposed to ask rather than assume.

"Could you put a Sweet'N Low in there?" Mr. Danvers asks me, just as he has the previous four evenings. He is a wispy-haired gentleman boasting what appears to be a full set of natural teeth, and he seems obsessed with this sugar substitute.

I nod, knowing what to expect, and tear the tiny pink packet. He likes when I stir it into his coffee for him, and I don't mind. As I have already learned from my time with Aunt Evelyn, routines are important for the elderly.

"Sweeeet'N Low," he croons while I mix in the granules.

Not everyone speaks to me or even acknowledges my presence, but I don't take offense. To some, I am a jailer in their prison, marked as an enemy by my white pants, sea-green Briar Creek Manor uniform top, and young face. To others, I am just the help, and that's fine too.

Who knows who they all were in their previous lives? Despite the cleanliness, caring, and efficiency of Briar Creek Manor, it still might not feel like home to those who have maintained their minds. Others—residents who have started to fall into dementia—just don't understand why they are in this place with all of these old people. It is sad.

I am relieved that Aunt Evelyn can still take care of herself. It breaks my heart to see the empty stares of so many once-productive citizens.

A bony hand clenches around my wrist while I am pouring Mrs. Mayfield's tea. I steady my hand before spilling more than a drop.

"Gloria?" she asks.

This is always so awkward. Even though I have only worked a few shifts so far, several of the residents have mistaken me for someone else: a daughter, a friend, a sister.

"Sorry, no. It's only me, Callie." I point to my name tag and try to avoid speaking in a way that sounds patronizing. She is confused, but she is still an adult.

"Gloria, you've come back for me!" she says.

To my alarm, her eyes fill with tears. I don't know who Gloria is or where she went, but I am guessing she left several decades prior to today.

"Enjoy your meal." I walk away, hoping her sobs will subside.

Being a dietary aide can be emotionally stressful.

I am not ready to go back to Aunt Evelyn's after work. Needing a breather from the elderly, I drive the short distance to Nan's Coffee Shop and Bakery, craving that which is cheerful, shiny, and new, not to mention my vices of sugar and caffeine.

As a bonus, the hot guy is behind the counter. He smiles, and this somehow makes me feel like an idiot once again.

"Large skim cappuccino?" he asks, showing that maybe I did make an impression on him, after all. "And a cookie, was it?"

"Yes, on the coffee, but I'm going to go with a piece of that blackberry cobbler." I am somewhat proud of myself for not stuttering or pretending like I eat celery all the time. "It's been a rough day."

"Oh?" he murmurs in reply, punching my order into the register and scooping out the piece of cobbler in one fluid move. He has skills, this guy, but I can't tell if he really cares or not, so I don't elaborate, and he doesn't ask me to. "I'll call you when it's ready."

"Thanks," I say, still awkward and out of practice talking to people my age.

How will he call me when he doesn't know my name? I consider telling him, but I somehow have enough sense to avoid humiliating myself further. He would probably think I am trying to ask him out or something.

A few minutes later, I have my treat and Hester by my side, making me far more relaxed than I have been all day. I am only a few pages into my reading session when I glance up.

A familiar face looms over me.

"Hey," Brian, the dry cleaner, says. He is sipping some kind of foamy, pink, whipped cream beverage which contrasts drastically with the severity of his black attire. "I guess you got the job?"

He has noticed my giveaway: the ugly uniform and blockish, rubbery nurse's shoes I am wearing. Not only is the outfit hideous, but I probably have more than one smear of pureed steak somewhere on my clothing. Still, it is nice that he asked.

"Yeah, I did. Thank you for telling me about it! The job's not bad, and the money's pretty good."

He kind of just stands there for a moment.

"Glad I could help," he says finally. "Like I said, it's pretty boring here for us city folk." He smirks and does a long, elaborate eye roll at Nan's jolly décor.

There is a thin line between being friendly and desperate, but it is just this guy, Brian, who I am definitely not interested in, so I go for it. "Want to join me?"

"Sure." He grins and sits.

I get the feeling he was waiting for an invitation.

"Were you on your way somewhere?"

He is holding a bag and was probably stopping by for takeout.

"Just home. I picked up some treats. My grandpa and I both have a sweet tooth."

"Me too." I gesture to my half-eaten cobbler.

Maybe I should stick to talking with old people; this feels downright painful. Have I forgotten how to make conversation with people my age? Next, we will be talking about the weather, or—hopefully not—the crops or something. Not that I know anything about crops, but that is probably what people in Deerville must do for small talk.

"Hey!" His face lights up when he notices my book. "Have you read this before?"

"No, I'm just getting into it. Required summer reading for AP Lit next year. I'm trying to be productive during my time here." It is a stupid thing to lie about, like I am ashamed to enjoy reading. I am taking that class, but I chose the book for pleasure rather than because it was a homework requirement, which it is not.

Brian picks up the book and runs his hand over the cover. "I read it last year in AP Lang. I guess we're both a couple of nerds?"

"English is my best subject. I'm no slouch."

I don't consider myself a nerd—no pocket protector here, people. He is trying to bond or something. I have to admit, I am kind of impressed that he takes AP classes, or at least one.

The cash register guy walks by, and Brian says, "You won't catch that one reading a book. Dumb as a bag of hammers, but the girls seem to go for him." He punctuates this denouncement with a noisy slurp.

I have to smile at this. Girls always give guys a hard time about judging them based on looks, and I have fallen into the same trap.

"Oh, I don't know. He gave me the right change and everything, even if he didn't wow me with his scintillating conversation."

Am I flirting? It has been so long that I can't even tell.

Brian turns his attention back to the book. "So, I don't want to give anything away. You obviously know that Hester got herself all preggers and the mean old Puritans hate her for it. Did you meet Chillingworth yet? Isn't that a cool name? It's right up there with Miss Havisham."

He opens the book to check where I am. My yellowed newspaper clipping, which I am still using as a bookmark, flutters to the table and falls flat in front of him, headline up.

For a moment, he says nothing. Then, slowly and deliberately, he asks, "Why do you have this?"

He is not wrong to criticize my choice of bookmark. After all, the clipping looks musty and probably has silverfish guts on it.

"It was stuck in the book. I got it from Burke's."

Brian flattens out the clipping on the table with care, as if it is something important. "It's kind of weird that you're using a suicide article for a bookmark."

Is he super religious or something and about to accuse me of disrespecting the dead? I take a slow sip of my cappuccino and wish for the easy camaraderie of just moments before.

"You're right. Morbid. But I feel weird about throwing it away, you know? It's like that's her whole life, and she's gone, so it kind of feels disrespectful to not keep it, you know?"

"Yeah, okay," he says, not sarcastically, but the mood has changed. "What's weird is that she was, like, my grandpa's cousin. She was a lot older, so she was his babysitter, mostly, but they spent time together. What are the chances of me finding this article about my great- or third cousin or whatever? She was only a little older than us when she died, you know. And meanwhile, he's in his eighties. All those years she never got to live."

"Yeah." We sit in silence and think about the significance of this before I continue. "It was her choice, though. It's horrible that she thought she had no options, but I can't feel too bad for her when other people have died because they *had* to die. They didn't ask for cancer or a car accident, or whatever."

I gulp and try to make eye contact, but Brian keeps staring at the article.

"I'm not totally heartless, Brian. I think it's sad that she did it, but I also think it's selfish. Look at the people she hurt by choosing to end it, like your grandfather. And how about her baby? The baby never even got a chance to live."

"My grandpa said it had to have been an accident," Brian replies, meeting my gaze. "He said she'd never choose that for herself."

"Okay." What else can I say? "But think about it. She was pregnant and unmarried in a time when people really looked down upon that. And does it even matter now how she died? That was, like, eighty years ago. No one will ever know what she was thinking and why it happened. Not now, if they never figured it out then. It's just a sad situation."

"Eighty-one years. And you're right, but she was still a person.

And I know I never met her, but I *am* related to her, so she matters to me. My grandpa still talks about her sometimes—all these crazy situations at their grandparents' farm. Even though she was older, they were close because they were both only children. Like me. I don't even have cousins. Or parents, for that matter."

Another awkward moment. I feel guilty now for my lack of empathy, both for the girl, Betty, and for Brian himself.

"You're right. She was a person, and she does matter. I'm sorry your grandfather lost her."

Brian nods once and then does a kind of full body shudder, like he is pulling himself out of and away from his feelings. He stands up from the table and grabs his paper bag. "Listen, sorry I got so dark. I guess it's not a total surprise, right?" He flashes me a grin and points with his free hand to his macabre ensemble. "I need to get going, but I'll see you around, okay?"

"Sure."

Sadly, this is as close to a friend as I have made in Deerville. He is the only person with whom I have had anything resembling a normal conversation, even if things did get a little weird just now.

"Do you want this? Maybe to give your grandpa?" I try to hand him the clipping.

He considers it for a moment, furrowing his brow. "No, Callie. I think you should keep it."

With that, he turns and heads out, leaving me with the dregs of my coffee and the thoughts of this long dead girl who did or didn't choose to end things for herself and her unborn child.

CHAPTER

SIX

I am on early shift a few mornings later, and my role at breakfast is once again dining room duty: pour coffee, listen to Mr. Danvers recite his ode to Sweet'N Low, dodge butt pinches and swats from both old men and ladies alike. It is all part of the routine. Free from the watchful eyes of my super-conscientious fellow employees, I allow myself a bit of a mental walkabout, wondering about the residents' past lives and thinking about what I am missing back home.

Mrs. McPherson snaps me back to my present, though I am pretty sure she herself is stuck in the past. Her bony wrist lashes out at me with startling speed and strength, and she grabs my hand, causing me to slosh a little coffee from the pot.

Surprised, I let out a feeble gasp while I peel off her fingers.

"Who are you?" she demands, like the caterpillar in *Alice in Wonderland*—without the smoke but with a sense of urgency. Her eyes, cloudy with cataracts or glaucoma, are laser-focused on mine. "Why have you come here?"

I am used to this by now and go through the motions. "I'm Callie. I work here, Mrs. McPherson."

I set the coffee pot back on my cart and grab a cloth napkin to try to sop up the spill—a brown jellyfish already spreading its tentacles across the immaculate white tablecloth. Hawthorne's word *ignominy* flashes through my mind. He used it enough in the first few chapters of *The Scarlet Letter* to describe Hester's shame. I hope to avoid a browbeating for this sloppiness since it wasn't my fault.

"Should I pour you more coffee?"

"Callie? No, that's not right." But she breaks her gaze to touch the stain instead, seeming confused.

Whatever broke through to her, whatever powerful and vital thought from decades past, has dried up, while the coffee has not.

"Have a good day," I tell her.

She looks up at me with none of the interest from before.

After work, I head to the park before going back to Aunt Evelyn's. It is too hot to do anything athletic, and I didn't bring the right clothes anyway. I find a nice, secluded, shady spot under a tree and try to read, but the heat and the long day on my feet get the best of me...

A rustle...

I don't know how long I have been sleeping, but dusk has settled. The sun has dipped below the horizon. It is a miracle I still have my wallet and car keys after having left myself vulnerable. Then again, Deerville does feel pretty safe. I can't imagine that a thief would get very far here, and what would he do? Go on a spending spree at Ned's Hardware?

The rustle comes again, followed by a muted, girlish laughter. My body tenses.

Who is here? Am I being watched?

The low rumblings of a male voice.

I relax but become embarrassed after realizing what I am hearing.

A couple messing around.

I don't want to be present for what may come next, so I quietly gather my belongings and get to my feet, tiptoeing toward the parking lot.

A familiar-looking dark, shaggy head is ahead of me.

"Brian?" I call.

His back is turned away, but he swings around quickly. "Oh! Hi," he says, appearing a little flustered. "What are you doing here?"

I hold up my book, even though it is getting a little too dark to read. "I fell asleep," I explain. "And then I woke up from a noise."

"Oh." He rubs his shoe on the ground as if trying to dislodge a piece of gum. Brian seems off.

Is our conversation about the drowned girl still bothering him?

Still, he is one of the only people I know in town—and the friendliest at that—so I come out with it.

"What are you doing here? Don't parks close at dusk?"

I contemplate whether he is acting weird because maybe he is supposed to meet a girl or something. Perhaps the park becomes make-out central after the sun goes down.

He points to something in his hand I hadn't noticed before. Binoculars? Eww. No wonder he is rattled. Was he seriously spying on the couple making out?

"It's pretty geeky," he says.

"Geeky isn't the word—" I barely conceal my disdain, but Brian continues.

"There was a nighthawk sighting a few days ago," he says.

I have no idea what he is talking about, and this must show on my face, even in the dim lighting.

"I used to go birding with my dad when I was a kid, and I still get these bird alerts sometimes and go check them out."

Huh?

"You mean, like, bird watching?" I ask, remembering that Brian said he didn't have parents.

"Yeah, but sort of competitive. You try to 'capture' all these different birds in your journal. If you think you see it, you check for all the tell-tale markings and stuff." He points to one of the many pockets in his pants, where a slim volume peeks out. "It's not really very exciting, you know, sitting outside in the heat or cold or rain, just for a quick glimpse of a bird that you might not even see, but my dad was really into it, and it makes me feel close to him sometimes. Pretty lame, right? Like hunting, in a way, all the waiting, but the animal gets to live and your 'trophy' is just the knowledge that you've seen it."

"That's kind of cool—the hunt with no kill."

"My parents were like that. Nature lovers. We used to travel to all kinds of places and have these amazing adventures. I even went snorkeling in the Great Barrier Reef once."

He gazes off in the distance, as if he can see that happier time. It reminds me of Aunt Evelyn or one of the Briar Creek Manor residents looking back to their youth. But Brian is too young for his happiness to all be in the past.

"I thought I'd have so much more time with them, you know? I had just turned thirteen when they died. I was starting to do that whole annoying-teenager thing, complaining about everything and acting all aloof. I wish I could take it back, have a do-over."

I don't know what to say or where to look. Even though I am pretty pissed off at my parents for sending me here, I am grateful they are still living and breathing on this earth.

"I'm sure they knew you loved them," I say, feeling like it is not the right thing, but what on earth is?

"Yeah. I hope so. It's why I'm so good to my grandpa. I don't want him to ever be sorry he got stuck with me. He already lost everyone else." Brian looks up at me, his mouth set in a determined line. "Life goes on, though, right?"

Whatever black hole he opened into his personal history is now closed. He refuses to wallow in self-pity.

I am ashamed for thinking Brian was a pervert when he is just a sad guy missing his parents. "I hope you find your bird." I wave goodbye and head to my car.

Aunt Evelyn practically pounces on me when I get home, even though it is not quite 9:00. "Where were you?" She doesn't sound mad, but she was obviously worried.

"I'm sorry, Aunt Evelyn. I went to the park after work, and I sort of fell asleep for a while. I woke up, and it was getting dark."

"I need to know if you plan to go somewhere," she says, somewhat sternly.

I can imagine her as the schoolmarm she once was.

"It won't happen again," I say. "I ran into a friend after I woke up. Brian Spencer. Do you know him?"

"Oh, yes, that poor boy. He's a bit peculiar, but he's polite when I go to his grandfather's shop. I believe he's very good to his grandfather."

I can't imagine what items in Aunt Evelyn's simple wardrobe need to be dry cleaned, but I hold my tongue. Aunt Evelyn seems to approve of Brian, which makes me glad, knowing how she is disappointed by the youth of today. But then her sharper tone startles me.

"There's nothing untoward going on between you two, I hope?"

"No, Aunt Evelyn. We're just friends. He's like a brother or something to me."

This isn't quite true. I wouldn't say we are very close yet, and I don't even know what having a brother is like since I only have a sister. But there is definitely nothing going on with us. Even his alternative style is kind of growing on me a bit.

I decide to divert the subject away from romance—*completely* away.

"What happened to his parents?" I couldn't bring myself to ask Brian, even though he was talking about them, not wanting to pry or bring up painful memories.

"Car accident," she replies without fanfare, as if telling me what her favorite color is.

Maybe, at her age, death is never shocking and this is just one of countless unfortunate situations she has heard or read about during her long, long life.

"Now that you're home, are you ready for *Bonanza*?"

CHAPTER

SEVEN

My swimming suit looks more like a dress. I am reclining on a towel, like I am sunbathing beside Abbott Lake, but it is dark out, with only the thin luminescence of light. The full moon's reflection floats in the tranquility of the water.

Brian, stretched out on another towel near me, points at a bird, which must be his nighthawk. "Wait till I tell Dad!" he exclaims.

I remember his dad is dead.

In the background plays that song again, that "Moonlight Cocktail" one.

I calmly watch a figure step out of the lake. Dark hair covers her face, and a scarlet A has been stitched onto the bodice of a nightgown which clings to her like a second skin.

Brian points at her, just as he did to the nighthawk. "Look, Callie! Wait till I tell Grandpa!" He seems excited.

My body is covered in a cold sweat when I wake with a gasp. I swear I can still smell the earthiness of the lake. It is a reflex to look at my phone for the time, maybe to check how many more hours before the safe haven of daylight seeps into my room.

Yep, it is 12:17 again.

I close my eyes and try to will the morning to come. The house is too quiet, too old, and I long for the comfort of my own bed and family.

Since I am not working today, I allow myself a good "lie in," as they say in England—at least in the books I read. My sleep, when it finally returned, was restless, but at least it was dreamless after that initial chilling scene by the lake.

When I finally come downstairs out of hunger, I haven't even brushed my hair or teeth, let alone changed out of my pajamas. Therefore, I am somewhat mortified to see that Aunt Evelyn has a guest.

It is Brian, standing ramrod straight. Apart from his dyed-looking black hair and ear gauges, he is dressed like any preppy guy in a polo shirt and khaki shorts. I almost sigh in relief—he is wearing a pair of beaten-up sneakers rather than boat shoes. It would have been way too much.

I cross my arms over my chest, self-conscious of my lack of bra, and look at him in confusion. "Hi...?"

Brian is not surprised to see me since he knows I am living here, but he seems a little put out all the same. "Hi, Callie. Didn't I mention that I was coming by today?"

"No." I am still ill at ease. And what does Aunt Evelyn think of this exchange and the fact that I am dressed—or not dressed—as I am, considering our conversation last night?

He picks up a garbage bag off the floor as an explanatory prop. "It's donation day. I do it every couple of months. I go around collecting used clothing. We clean it, and then we donate it all to the Red Cross. My grandpa has me make stops at all the"—he glances at Aunt Evelyn, tongue-tied—"the houses of those people who have a harder time getting out by themselves."

Aunt Evelyn makes a little snorting sound, as if to show she is extremely capable of getting out of the house, but at least Brian is trying to be respectful.

"Well, it sounds like you're a good citizen," I say. The conversation is weirdly stilted in front of Aunt Evelyn for some reason.

A graduation requirement pops into my head: community service hours. I can probably get Brian's grandpa or the donation center to sign off on it. If not, at least it will give me something to do other than watch TV all day.

"Can I join you? I'd like to be a good citizen myself." I look at Aunt Evelyn sitting and stirring her decaf coffee. After the scolding of last night, I want to make sure she is cool with me being spontaneous. "That is, if it's okay with you."

She raises her eyebrows and shrugs her slight shoulders. "Certainly. Maybe you'll meet some of my old friends. Please let them know that we are kin and give them my regards."

I get myself together upstairs, skipping the shower but at least deodorizing and putting on some of my own preppy-looking clothes. When I go to grab a granola bar, Brian shakes his head.

"Just trust me on this—there will be food."

Brian drives us in an old Chevy pickup truck that isn't fitting for either his regular look or his new one. I imagine him in suspenders and a straw hat, hauling bales of hay. After I have buckled my seatbelt, I ask him about his outfit.

"Well, you know, I'm dealing with all old folks today," he says without even a hint of defensiveness. He backs out of Aunt Evelyn's driveway. "I try to tone it down a bit. People around here aren't like they were back in Philly, you know? People just expect everything to be so cookie cutter here."

"I've noticed that too. Not exactly a lot of diversity of any type."

"They're really big on rules and routines too. Graduate high school. Commute to the local college while living at home. Get married and have kids after graduation. Work your forty-hour week. Stay in Deerville until you die from natural causes or boredom."

Brian pauses to sigh.

"Did you notice that everyone has two kids here? Not one and not three. Two. And nobody gets divorced. It's weird. This one customer, Mrs. Jenkins? Her husband left town for another woman, supposedly. She lasted all of two months before she left town herself. It's like we're stuck in another era—a divorce is scandalous!"

"I didn't notice. I haven't exactly been a social butterfly since I got here," I reply.

He seems to be taking this personally somehow.

Brian stares at the road as if he is pulling complicated maneuvers on the highway instead of driving in the middle of nowhere with no other cars in sight. I glance away, taking in the lush farmland and cotton-ball clouds in the sky.

"They didn't really know what to make of me when I got here. They were okay with my grandpa. Your wife and kid can die, I guess, but you're abnormal if your parents die. Not like I had any say in it. I've never really fit in here. I just do my own thing. I don't care what anyone thinks."

This last sentence sounds a bit defensive, making me think it is not entirely true. We drive in silence for several minutes.

By the time we pull into a long driveway, he changes his tone. "Okay, time to put on my nice face." It is the only face I have seen from him, but apparently, there is bitterness hidden underneath his smile.

The house must have been magnificent once, but time has taken its toll, chipping away at the stone front. The garden, though overgrown with long grasses and wildflowers, retains some of its grandeur through the majesty of the sleepy cherry tree in its center. I step onto the uneven porch, hoping the boards won't cave in under our weight.

"This may take a while." Brian brings the heavy knocker to the door. His dark eyes lighten to golden brown in the sun. His mood seems airier as well. He points out various birds to me while we wait. "Look! An ibis!"

"I know what an ibis is," I say, annoyed. But I quickly contort my face back into something resembling a smile when the slow shuffle of elderly feet comes our way.

A plump, ancient woman peers at us through the door. Her sparse eyebrows raise while she checks us out. "Brian! So nice to see you!" she declares when she recognizes him, as if he is dropping by unexpectedly instead of having prearranged this visit. "Please, come in!"

Brian, ever the gentleman, introduces me. "Mrs. Winchester, this is my friend, Callie Quinn. She's helping me out today. You know her great-great-aunt, Evelyn Reynolds."

"Evelyn! Yes, of course. Why, it's been years since we saw each other! She was ahead of me in school, but I was friendly with the older girls."

She looks just as old as Aunt Evelyn, so I am somewhat tickled by her vain declaration that she is younger. Does it even matter at that age? What, she's like eighty-six or eighty-seven instead of eighty-nine? Didn't older women wear their ages like badges of honor after a certain point? My mother turned forty a while back and made a huge deal about feeling old, but I didn't think that would last forever.

Mrs. Winchester's hand disappears into one of the voluminous pockets of her house dress. "Let me get a good look at you, and then I'll get us all some tea," she says, putting on her glasses. "Oh."

She exhales after expressing her single syllable.

I am not sure how to take this assessment of my appearance. Good thing I at least took the time to brush my hair!

Brian steps in, offering a lifeline. "So, Mrs. Winchester, I don't suppose you have some of your famous scones? Callie, they're amazing, and she uses fresh blueberries from her garden."

"I'm sorry, dear," Mrs. Winchester says to me, her mouth forming into a more benign expression. "You don't look much like your aunt. You just surprised me a little. I didn't mean to be rude."

"No, it's fine. Aunt Evelyn's kind of far removed from me in terms of genetics, so that's why we look so different." It is true. I feel like an Amazon woman when I stand next to her.

Aunt Evelyn says she has always been petite, but she has lost even more height in her later years, and she is slender as well. I am only average in height, with an athletic build, but I practically look like another species next to her, especially with my darker coloring.

"You look strong." Mrs. Winchester pinches my thigh, a move I would find completely inappropriate and bizarre if not for all my recent experiences with the elderly. "Nice and firm. You might not know this, but Evelyn used to be quite the athlete as well."

"Really?" This is news to me. Aunt Evelyn is very strict about her exercise routine, but it is not exactly intense, so I struggle to picture this version of her.

I follow Mrs. Winchester closely through the narrow hallway containing tremendous stacks of newspapers and need to back up when she swings around.

"Baseball!" she shouts, reliving a long-ago memory. "She was really something. My sisters and I would watch the older girls play. Could she ever hit a ball! What strength in those arms! Those were some lovely memories. I cherish those afternoons even more now that they have all passed."

She says this solemnly but without regret, and I think again how death seems less jarring to the elderly.

The kitchen, with its large bay window and cheery dandelion walls, is surprisingly bright and tidy compared to the rest of the house, at least from what I have seen. She motions for us to sit and bustles around.

I can't help but be intrigued by the over-the-top display in front of us, especially since I am starving.

Mrs. Winchester has laid out an elaborate blue and white floral tea set. A mountain of scones is arranged on the matching trays, and I get the distinct feeling that Brian's community service is about far more than picking up donations.

It is obvious Mrs. Winchester wants, or even needs, the company.

Three hours later, though our donations are few, we are full of tea and various baked goods from the handful of houses we visited.

"I can't eat another bite," I complain, buckling myself back into the passenger seat.

"It comes with the territory." Brian smiles at me, all traces of his earlier surliness drowned with weak Earl Grey tea. "You did great. I don't know how many other kids our age would be able to handle this morning. You were really awesome with them."

I roll my eyes in mock annoyance, but I actually had fun. "I seriously can't believe I hung out with old people all morning on my day off from the nursing home. And it's crazy how everyone we visited was a widow. I'm surprised they're not beating down your grandpa's door."

"Yeah, he's definitely had some interest from the ladies since I've been living with him. He told me that my grandmother is the only woman he's ever loved. He says he doesn't have room for anyone else now. I don't know if you've ever seen someone with dentures try to flirt before, but it's kind of scary." He glances sideways at me. His eyes are twinkling. "You want me to drop you off, or do you want to meet him?"

"Sure." I don't have anything better to do anyway, and I am curious. What is one more old person? I'm a pro. "Meet him, that is."

So, we drive in the direction of town, toward the mystery man Brian thinks of so highly.

CHAPTER

EIGHT

Brian and his grandpa live just a block behind their shop. It is one of the huge Victorian homes which pepper the streets of Deerville.

Each house is long and deep. Some are stately manors, while others have fallen into neglect, with faded paint, rotted boards, and broken windows. Some homeowners have gone to such trouble to maintain their property, and it must drive them crazy when other neighbors have done nothing. Maybe it is a metaphor for the lives of the people in this town.

Brian's house is sort of in the middle.

Well, it literally is.

To the left, an enormous freshly painted brick structure would have fooled me into thinking it was new construction if not for the tell-tale style. And to the right lies a rather derelict house with crumbling latticework, a junky chain link fence, and a bunch of propane tanks in the yard.

Though the yellow plaster siding with white trim of 3 Butterfly Lane could use a good wash and some tending to its garden, it is neither grand nor dilapidated. Its rounded porch and modest columns give the look of elegance without ostentation. A couple of hanging baskets and two rocking chairs are a far cry from the lush garden on one side and clutter of wind chimes and grimacing gnome statues of the neighboring houses, but I definitely like this one the best.

"You have a beautiful house," I say to Brian. Although I love my own, it has none of the character of this one. Mine is a replica of the others in my neighborhood, with their carpeted basements and granite countertops. There is nothing which makes it unique.

Brian opens the unlocked, intricately carved wooden door, and we go inside. I run my fingers over the wall. There is some sort of raised design—a repeating fleur-de-lis pattern—all over the bottom half. Though just as old-looking, with its high ceilings and chandelier, the house is far more striking than Aunt Evelyn's.

Brian catches me noticing the details. "The house has been the same for my entire life and probably for much of my grandpa's. He's lived here his whole life. Nothing ever changes around here. Same everything. Just fewer people since, you know, dying runs heavily in my family."

"Heel, boy," says a voice from the next room.

The man shuffling in, with his hand on the back of an enormous yellow Lab, reminds me of many of the residents at the nursing home: white hair combed neatly over a freckled scalp, stooped shoulders, bulbous nose, sagging eyelids. When he looks up at me, though, his brown eyes are still full of life, interest, and clarity. He extends a hand toward me.

"Burt Spencer. You must be Brian's new friend. He's told me about you." His voice is gravelly but kind, catching just a bit, as if he hasn't used it in a while, rusty like the hinges on the door I just walked through.

I shake his hand. My small, smooth one is swallowed in his gnarled, rough paw, and I think how Brian greeted me. Despite age and style, grandfather and grandson have the same brown eyes and impeccable manners.

"Hi, I'm Callie. My great-great-aunt is Evelyn Reynolds." I turn to Brian. "You never told me you had a dog." More shocking is, I haven't seen any evidence of this great blond beast's fur all over Brian's black wardrobe.

He shrugs. "There are lots of things you don't know about me. This is Willy."

"He's an old guy like me," Mr. Spencer says. "His hearing's definitely going. Just last year, he would've come in barking up a storm if you kids came through the door. I think I heard you before he did." He pulls Willy's muzzle away from its perusal of my leg and scratches the dog under the chin.

"It's okay. I have a dog too. In Cagney." When I reach to pet Willy, I feel a pang of longing for Priscilla, my German Shepherd mix.

Before I got so busy with high school, I used to take her for walks every day and lounge on the couch, snuggling. I even used to paint her nails. Now it has been a month since I have even seen her, her slobbery kisses fading like a distant memory. At least I know I am going back, to her and everything else in my life.

A plume of fur seems to shoot off Willy's back from all the petting, and Brian laughs. The dog stretches and collapses in a golden heap on the floor.

"It's a relief I'm not wearing black for once. My grandpa says he should buy stock in lint rollers."

"Donations in the truck?" Mr. Spencer asks, and Brian nods. He walks us into the kitchen and gestures for us to sit. "Want anything, or are you full of tea and all that?"

"Yup—stuffed. Just wanted to take a short break. I'll drop the bags off at the shop in a bit."

It dawns on me that neither of them is at their store, and no one else works there.

"Are you closed today?" I ask. "Isn't it Monday?"

"Yes, but it's the first Monday of the month. We close the store, pick up the donations, clean them, and take them to the needy. It's been my practice for over sixty years. It's one of the reasons folks keep coming back to me instead of driving to the fancier place in the next town." Mr. Spencer looks sideways at his grandson. "The boy here might not always appreciate Deerville, but it's a good place with decent people who value community."

Brian doesn't appear peeved, exactly, but he is up to something.

"Grandpa, you didn't always think so. What about when you were a kid and your cousin died? The 'community' didn't seem to worry about her very much. Tell her about that. Callie's the one who found that clipping."

The spark in Mr. Spencer's eyes dulls. "My cousin's death was a tragedy, Callie. She was young and full of promise. I'll never know what happened at the lake, and I am saddened by that. But I won't turn against this town, not now and not ever. It's quite a coincidence that you happened to find that article, and I'll admit that it brought up some feelings when Brian told me, but it's ancient history. Case closed."

Brian glares, his eyes even darker than normal under his furrowed brow. "Grandpa, the case is *not* closed. Even if she was pregnant, you said she'd never kill herself. You said it must have been an accident, but how could it be if she knew how to swim? And why would she be at the lake by herself late at night?"

When we talked about Betty before, Brian seemed interested in preserving her memory as a non-suicide, but I didn't think he had any theories on what had happened. I don't want to offend Mr. Spencer in any way, though, so I decide to keep my thoughts to myself for now. Later, when it is just Brian and me, I will have to find the right words.

Mr. Spencer sighs.

"Son. We've been through this. No one in this town would have hurt her, not even with the scandal. Let it go. And you're not the one who lost her. I accept my grief, just as I always have."

At this, Brian looks up at his grandfather, only a crumb of rebellion left.

"Show her," he says, his voice soft, careful to preserve civility.

He respects Mr. Spencer and doesn't want to upset him. They have both been touched with so much death and abandonment.

"Show her the picture. Show her Betty."

Mr. Spencer pauses, looking from Brian to me, and acquiesces with a simple, curt nod that ripples his jowls. He gets up heavily from his chair with a stern look on his face.

Brian and I remain silent while he is gone. I have so many questions, but it is not the right time. Brian is hunkered over the wooden kitchen table, looking far older than his seventeen years. He no longer resembles the cheerful good Samaritan who visits old people and collects clothing for the poor, and I wonder about this chameleon-like quality. Brian pushes the dark hair off his forehead, pulling it into a point, brooding, and I notice a long, jagged scar.

He catches me looking, even though his eyes seem unfocused. "Yeah, I was in the car too." His voice is hollow. "Don't worry. It doesn't hurt when Voldemort's around or anything."

His joke falls flat. I have nothing to say, although I am cold despite the coziness of the kitchen. It is bad enough he lost his parents, but I can't possibly imagine the terror of witnessing their deaths. I busy myself by looking at my feet.

Mr. Spencer walks back in with a shoebox in his hands, holding it like he is carrying something breakable, something precious. He places the box on the table.

"This is Betty."

For a moment, I think he means her ashes are inside. My lack of poker face must give me away.

He quickly says, "No! I mean, these are her things."

I don't exactly want to intrude on their family tragedy, yet I sort of do. It has been weird, finding the article like I did and having those dreams. Betty is about to become far more real for me, and I take a moment to remember that she was this nice man's cousin, not just an interesting character from a book I am reading.

Mr. Spencer waves his hand impatiently. He wants me to open the box. It is old and worn but looks cardboard, and my guess is, it is from way back then. The green advertisement is faded, yet I can clearly make out the words "Brenda's Dry Goods" on the box. I still don't know what dry goods are, but I have passed the sun-bleached sign on Main Street.

Brian sits with eyes cast down. I don't know why he seems angry or with whom he is mad, but he is.

I open the box—a portal to this poor girl's short life.

What could end up in a shoebox to represent me? Photographs? Report cards? Some poems I have written? My iPhone? I have no idea, not wanting to imagine my life snuffed out like hers was.

On the top is a black-and-white photograph, now tinted brownish yellow with age. It is small, less than a four-by-six print, but it is a close-up, a formal portrait. Betty is dressed in a shirt with puffy sleeves and a striped collar sticking out. She is neither smiling nor frowning. A simple crucifix hangs around her neck, under the collar but on top of the fabric.

Her lipstick-darkened lips are pursed into a slight smile. Her dark, shoulder-length hair, parted on the side, is half pinned back in floating waves. What sort of old-fashioned hair contraption was required for her to achieve those results?

Her eyes are what draw me in, though. Dark, wide, and guileless, they stare openly at the camera. She is innocent, vibrant, and beautiful. I try to replace this picture of youthful vivacity with the images I have seen in my dreams: her limp body, her vacant eyes.

"You're probably wondering why I have that picture in a box instead of on the wall," Mr. Spencer says. "Good question. My wife hung all the pictures in the living room, and I only rediscovered this box a couple of years ago, after she died. I need a frame, and then I'll add her to the wall with the others."

He points toward the living room, where I assume he displays the faces of his various deceased loved ones.

"I should have taken better care of this. After Betty died, her parents—my aunt and uncle—disposed of all of her belongings. I was just a boy, so I didn't understand why they would act that way. My parents didn't tell me about the baby. Secrets like that were swept under rugs back then. It destroyed Betty's parents to the point that they wouldn't even grieve for her. Such a shame."

Mr. Spencer looks off in the distance, as if back to that day. I almost say something to try and offer comfort of some sort, but Brian catches my gaze and shakes his head—a signal to let his grandfather continue his musings.

"This box, along with all of her clothes, was left out for the trash collectors. My father brought this home. No matter what she had done—pregnancy, maybe suicide—she was still his niece and my cousin, and her belongings shouldn't have been carted off to a landfill somewhere. My father never forgave his sister for that, not that he told her. I remember seeing it when I was a boy and needed some way to hold on to her, but then he put it up in the attic, where it stayed for many decades. To this day, I don't know if she put this together or if her parents just threw her possessions into this box."

"She's beautiful," I say, although there is so much more I can't articulate.

Betty was obviously more than a pretty face and a scandalous demise. She cared for her younger cousin, and she had dreams of becoming a nurse. I hope to learn more about her as we go through the box.

"She reminds me of you," Brian says. "The dark hair, obviously, but something else too. I can't put my finger on it."

Mr. Spencer narrows his eyes at me. "You do favor her, Callie.

How interesting. I hope that doesn't make you uncomfortable that we're saying this."

"No, not really." And it is true. It is even a little exciting in a way. I had no idea what she looked like until now, but she seems so familiar to me. I guess because I "saw" her in my dreams.

"Do you want to continue?" he asks, and I nod.

Mr. Spencer places the photograph to the side. He pulls out the rest of the items, arranging each on the table in front of us: movie ticket stubs, a few greeting cards, what looks like a journal or sketchbook, a set of earrings, a pair of fancy leather gloves, something knitted, and a handful of photographs.

Despite my dreams and my interest, Betty is more than a fascination to fill my time. As much as I crave information, her memory belongs to the old, sad-looking man sitting before me. I want nothing more than to read the greeting cards from people who must have been dear to her and rifle through all the pictures, to look at her sketches, if that is what they are. But I hold myself back as much as possible, threading my fingers together to force myself not to touch all that is in front of me. But then I notice something.

"It's a baby blanket!" Although it is in a ball, I recognize it for what it is because I helped my mom shop for a baby shower gift for one of her coworkers a few months ago. I can't help myself and grab it. White with a green trim. Three rabbits embroidered in the corner. "Don't you see? It's proof that she didn't kill herself!"

"I never believed that she did," her cousin says, loyal after all these years.

It doesn't take Nancy Drew to put these pieces together. "She knew she was pregnant, or she wouldn't have made this. And if she wanted to die, she also wouldn't have made this. Why make a blanket for a baby you know will never be born?"

Brian appears unimpressed, and he glowers at me. "This still doesn't help us figure out what happened. Why did she go to the lake at night, and how did she drown, if she actually accepted that she was unmarried and pregnant? Who was there with her? Who killed her?"

"Brian, no one is saying she was killed," Mr. Spencer says. "Don't get away from the facts."

Brian stands up. "Fact: She was unmarried and pregnant, which was a huge issue back then. Fact: She was accepted to nursing school, which shows she had planned a future. Fact: She knew how to swim. You said so yourself. Fact: She freaking made a baby blanket, which shows she was getting ready for a baby! What signs point to an accident, Grandpa? Callie, look at her book! Somebody killed her!"

I glance at Mr. Spencer, who grants his permission with a nod, though his eyes are heavy and his lips unsmiling. This whole thing pains him, yet he understands it is important to Brian, who never even knew her.

I reach for the volume, which has been covered in fabric and decorated with a variety of laces, ribbons, knitted flowers, and costume jewelry. It is quite ornate, suggesting the importance of what might be inside. But upon opening it, I am both disappointed and relieved that it is not a diary. As much as part of me wants to know everything about her, it would somehow feel wrong to be privy to Betty's secret thoughts.

What I find are sketches, and they are pretty good. Along with animals, trees, and flowers, she had also captured a couple of portraits.

"Is this you?" I ask, coming upon a young boy hauling a bucket toward waiting chickens.

While I don't know too much about drawing, having only taken basic art classes, I can tell she had some talent, with her shading and perspective. It made the young Mr. Spencer stand out as the focal point amongst the laborers she captured in the background.

"Life on our grandparents' farm," Mr. Spencer says. His smile barely touches his lips, but it is there all the same. "I did the work, and she sat and drew. Something seemed a bit off there."

And then I find the sketch that makes me sad: I recognize the lake. Abbott Lake, where she drowned.

In her drawing, it looks peaceful, just like when I came across it while running. There is some sort of bird near it and the beech tree, smaller in her depiction than it is now. A man or teenage boy sits in a relaxed pose, with his back turned to the artist, presumably enjoying the sunset. Maybe he is the baby's father, but he could have been a friend, relative, or even a figment of her imagination, conjured from nothing and adding to the serenity of the scene.

Betty's sketch exudes happiness. Could this prove that the lake was a place she went to be at peace with herself? That might explain why she was there that night, especially with the knowledge of her illicit pregnancy.

In between various drawings are a number of lists: books she read and movies she watched, along with brief but insightful thoughts about each one. Maybe she could have been a reviewer in another life.

Native Son—terrifying yet eye-opening. Would Deerville even recognize the cultural significance? Do they understand even the tiniest concept of race? I will never forget that scene with the furnace. Bigger Thomas is a product of small-mindedness.

I read it in tenth grade and totally agree.

Of Mice and Men—is this the saddest book ever written? Somewhere, Lennie is on that farm, petting his rabbits. Heartbreaking.

And gasp...

The Scarlett Letter—Hester is the strongest female protagonist, selflessly sacrificing her reputation, but to what purpose?

There is more on that one, but I stop reading—spoiler alert, Betty!

She could easily be here, talking to me as a friend in my English class, rather than a dead stranger from decades past. What would she think of some of the more modern literature I have read? I definitely can't imagine her going for the *Twilight* "nonsense," as Mr. Burke called it, but I bet she would have enjoyed the hell out of some *Harry Potter*.

"She read *The Scarlett Letter*," I say to Brian, pointing at the entry.

"There's more." He waits.

The pages have more sketches, as well as quotes and poems she transcribed, some of which are in a different language. None seem original, as far as I can tell, since she has written names next to the titles of each. Not a plagiarist, this chick.

Then I get to the numbers.

02   50.29.39.39.23.34   15.29.34.99.23.28   20.99.14   99.65   02.12
17.44.77.12.44.02.39.12   28.65.   02   29.28   39.23.34
02.39.34.65.77.65.12.34.65.74   02.39   99.02.28;   17.65.77.99.29.17.12
02.39   29.39.23.34.99.65.77   88.02.15.65,   29.39.74   23.39.88.14
02.15   20.65   20.65.77.65   15.77.65.65.   02.34
20.23.44.88.74   33.65   29   33.65.34.77.29.14.29.88.

"What's this?" I ask, but I already have an idea.

"I don't know, but it's something." Mr. Spencer's expression gives away nothing about how he feels. It is simply blank.

"What do you think?" Brian's curiosity is almost rabid. This is what he has been waiting for me to see.

"I bet it's a code. A cryptogram." If there is one thing I have used my brain power on this summer, it is solving puzzles.

My mission in those early, pre-job days in Deerville was to solve each puzzle in the newspaper, no matter how long it took—a distraction from Aunt Evelyn's endless syndicated episodes of *Magnum, P.I.* and the like. It helped me feel like I was using my brain for something. Every day, I did that stupid Cryptoquip by trial and error, even though the secret messages were mostly just puns and bad jokes. I am used to letter cryptograms rather than numbers, but this has to be one.

Maybe I am about to grow my own Tom Selleck moustache; that is how close I think I am to solving this case.

"Look at the punctuation. She uses a period at the end of each sentence, and there's also commas and a semicolon. All these numbers equate to letters. We just need to figure out which is which. Look at the small words—the one- and two-letter combinations. '02' has to be either A or I, which would make '02.12' either 'am,' 'an,' or 'is.' I'm pretty confident I can figure it out, if you want." I look straight at Mr. Spencer since he is the one who can grant me permission. "I don't know if you want to figure out what she was saying. There's a reason she coded it, like she knew someone would read it and wanted to keep it private."

The king of nonchalance, Mr. Spencer shrugs his shoulders. "What does it hurt? Try to crack it, Callie. I'm sure Brian has tried, and he must not have figured it out because the boy can't keep a secret for the life of him."

He smiles in response to Brian's scowl. I take a couple of photos with my phone to decipher later.

Brian shrugs in a visual echo of his grandfather. "Okay, yeah, that's true. I thought it was a code, but I didn't get it. I guess my brain isn't wired that way. I feel like it's the only clue she's given. Maybe she's writing about the pregnancy? Maybe she says something about the father." He sounds almost hungry.

"I keep telling him that it gets us nowhere. What if someone *did* kill my cousin? How could we prove it? And whoever would have done it is an even older man than me, which means he's probably dead or in a nursing home by now. And who knows who their killer is far enough in advance to write about it? Betty was no one's fool, so I can't imagine that she possibly would have walked to her death if she suspected anything was wrong." He sighs in resignation.

Brian sits down again but is still fidgety. "Do you think you can figure it out? Because it's driven me crazy."

"How long have you two been talking about this?" I ask boldly, knowing I probably shouldn't be interfering in family business.

"When did you show me this, Grandpa? A year ago? Two? I never heard about Betty growing up, but why would I? Everyone's so guarded in my family. Well, everyone was, and he still is." He jerks his thumb toward Mr. Spencer. It is clear he is again acknowledging his family tragedy.

I guess it is right there with him every day, a blight he can't block out.

"Yes, about that. Brian wanted to know about my experiences growing up, so I told him about Betty. My line has been largely childless, so relatives are few and far between." He says this simply and without regret. These are just the facts, ma'am.

I contrast this with the raucous family gatherings which I have always been a part of. Kids screaming and fighting, uncles getting sloshed, everyone talking at the same time...These Thanksgivings and Christmases have driven me crazy on multiple occasions, but I have enjoyed my loud, annoying, insane-in-the-membrane family too. It is a far cry from this rather grim twosome.

"Do you mind if I take a picture of some of her other things, like her drawings and her photograph? I think it would help me understand her better."

Mr. Spencer nods his assent—quite the nonverbal communicator—and flips through the sketchbook. "She's pretty good, isn't she? I used to think she should be an artist instead of a nurse. Not that anyone from around these parts ever went to one of those art schools. And, of course, she didn't get to be either of those things."

I say my goodbyes and leave him there with a dead girl's possessions, pieces of a puzzle we will most likely never solve.

CHAPTER

NINE

Brian stays mostly silent while he drives me home. He is not quite the guy I thought he was—a friendly face in an environment that, while not hostile, hasn't exactly been warm or welcoming.

It is not as if I have been going up to random people my age and starting conversations. I am not that desperate, and I have always been a little introverted and desirous of some solitude. Still, though, considering I work with some people my age and am pretty much a regular by now at one of the few local establishments where young people go, it is not like anyone else besides Brian has bothered reaching out to me.

He has a lot more darkness than I thought. Even though his outward alternative appearance is a big clue as to how he may feel inside, my initial interactions with him focused more on levity than the serious demeanor he seems to project of late. Then again, he is entitled to his feelings and gloominess, more so than anyone else I know.

Maybe it is a sign of his friendship for me that he feels he can let his guard down, especially when he just accused the members in his family of keeping theirs up.

"Hey...Sorry I've been a little, you know, intense today," he says, as if reading my thoughts. Brian keeps his eyes on the road. "It's hard to wear that mask of friendliness to the old folks and then have all this other stuff inside me."

"'We wear the mask that grins and lies,'" I quote from the famous Paul Laurence Dunbar poem. Maybe that's not quite the right sentiment to throw at him when he is obviously having a day, so I quickly retreat. "Not that I'm saying you're lying about anything. I just mean the mask part."

He sort of laughs and smiles, finally glancing over at me. Go figure that this super serious poem could lighten the mood.

"'It hides our cheeks and shades our eyes,'" he quotes back.

There's our connection: we bond in our nerdiness. I guess he was right about me being a nerd.

He pauses so long that I think he might be relapsing to silence, so I entertain myself by staring out the window at a cloud which starts out looking like a fish but morphs into a car when we get closer. It is an isolation thing: I am always good at occupying my mind, accustomed to long periods of quiet.

"I'm really glad to have met you, Callie. You're probably the only other person in Deerville who knows that poem. In seventh grade, before, back in Philly, my English teacher gave us a list of poems to choose from, but almost everyone picked that one to recite because it was the shortest. She about tore her hair out, especially when almost everyone mispronounced 'myriad subtleties.' But, yeah, I get that whole mask thing."

"Me too."

Some people would probably say the different parts of themselves are hats they wear, but aren't they really masks? Act one way as a student, act another as an athlete, another as a daughter, another as a sister, another as a friend, another as an employee...But which version of me is most myself? Do I act differently alone? I have no idea. I am pretty sure, though, that I am myself around Brian. I am comfortable enough around him to not have to wear any sort of mask.

We don't discuss it further, but our remaining silence in the car is companionable, at least. Warmth toward Brian surges through me while I head back into Aunt Evelyn's.

I am sort of ready for some me time when I come in, after having to be "on" while collecting donations and going through the box with Mr. Spencer.

It is not like he told me to keep it secret, but it seems like it would be disloyal to share anything with Aunt Evelyn about the window I may get into Betty's life. I love Aunt Evelyn and all, but I know how she feels about girls with "loose morals," so I wouldn't feel right opening up to her about poor Betty, assuming I can crack the code and that there is anything of interest there anyway.

Aunt Evelyn seems chatty when I walk through the door. My code-breaking will have to wait. When I sit down on the couch in front of the blaring television, she does something unprecedented: she turns it off.

"Whom did you see? Where all did you go?" she asks eagerly.

I begin to tell her about the humdrum events of my morning and answer her various questions. Whether or not Mrs. Winchester still has that hideous sofa she has had forever. What everyone offered me to eat and drink. Who had a large amount of donations and who didn't.

It dawns on me that, even though they are roughly in the same age group and live in the same town, Aunt Evelyn probably hasn't seen these people in ages. That is why she craves information about them. Despite her telling me at the beginning of the summer that she goes to breakfast with friends as part of her schedule, she hasn't done that even once while I have been here. I haven't worked a Friday morning shift. She has been home for each one.

I gather up my courage, trying my best to be diplomatic. "Aunt Evelyn, when's the last time you actually saw any of them?"

She blinks hard. "Oh, goodness! I really don't know! I'm sure I saw Doris Winchester at the grocery store in the last few years, and Maude Tierney and I used to have breakfast on Fridays. I guess it has been a while! When you're old, time seems to go faster, and one doesn't always make time for having company, I suppose."

"It sounds like you miss them, Aunt Evelyn. Why don't you schedule one of your Friday breakfasts with them? They asked about you, and I'm sure they'd love to see you."

"Yes, I should," she says, but she is quiet about it.

Is it a matter of pride that she doesn't want to be the one to reach out? It doesn't sound like there has been any sort of falling out, but maybe the friendships just drifted apart over the years.

Perhaps her seclusion, full of TV and crossword puzzles, became more of a comfort than socializing with other people. Or maybe these ladies were just casual acquaintances with whom she never enjoyed strong friendships in the first place, connected only by being in the same age group.

She picks up the remote, signifying the discussion is over.

I go up to my room early, telling Aunt Evelyn my stomach is upset from something I ate. While I certainly packed away enough sugar, caffeine, and fat while visiting all those houses earlier in the day for it to be a plausible story, it is not true. It is just a white lie to spare her from the fact that I would rather be alone.

I do feel jazzed up, but it is less from caffeine—which I think I am practically immune to anyway—and more from excitement. This code is something I want to figure out.

I *need* to.

After copying the code in a notebook, I make sure to leave spaces in between the lines for trial and error. I rummage through dresser drawers to find a pencil, knowing I will need to correct myself over and over, just like I do when figuring out the Cryptoquip in the newspaper.

It is a little different than what I am used to, with the numbers instead of letters. The numbers run 01 to 99 instead of just 01 to 26. In theory, though, it should be as easy since one number will still only represent one letter.

Finally, I have it, with a handful of letters not used and therefore not coded.

A=29G= 12M= 28S= 12Y= 14
B=33H= 99N= 39T= 34Z= ?
C=50I= 20= 23U= 44
D= 74J= ?P= 17V= ?
E= 65K= ?Q= ?W= 20
F= 15 L= 88R= 77X= ?

I cannot fathom why he is pursuing me. I am not interested in him; perhaps in another life, and only if we were free. It would be a betrayal.

It is still cryptic, which is weird since I already had to figure out a code to get this far, but it suggests a classic story of betrayal: guy falls for his girlfriend's friend, but even if she wants him, she doesn't want to hurt her friend. My guess is, she resisted him but finally gave in...and got pregnant? Maybe she was ashamed and killed herself after all? Or maybe the guy did it, not wanting to own up to the responsibility or for the girlfriend to find out?

Even though Betty made the baby blanket, the shame and guilt of the betrayal might have been too much. Maybe the girlfriend did find out and drowned her friend. Or Betty could have gone to the lake to think about her predicament and drowned by accident. The possibilities aren't exactly endless, but there are still several.

It is a fragment at first, a tiny piece of the memory slipping to the surface, like water through a pinprick-sized leak in a bucket. Still, it sends goosebumps up my arms despite the muggy temperature of my room.

Just like the water, though, it keeps coming, more and more, no matter how much I strive to hold it back. And then it is all there, what I tried to suppress, flooding through me, pictures and words and feelings.

It was all so innocent. At least, it started that way. I always thought Derek was cute, but he was with Leila, my best friend, so we were just friends. He was funny and kind back then, and it wasn't weird at all when Mr. Summerfield assigned us to be partners in World Cultures class.

Derek was basically an extension of Leila. We had already spent tons of time together; she had just always been there too. I didn't like him like that.

Derek and I were putting the finishing touches on our collaborative research paper after working on it for weeks, happy and giddy since we were finally almost done.

We were hunched close together in my room, over my computer. Mom and Dad probably wouldn't have cared about Derek being in my room—he had been to the house before with Leila. They knew he was her boyfriend and merely my friend, but they were out with Mia at some middle school concert and still weren't home.

"Done." I hit the print button with more than enough pressure for emphasis and clinked my coffee mug to his. "Nice work, pardner," I said in my best cowboy accent, which, of course, was terrible.

"You're really something, Callie Quinn. Do you know that?" The sun had long since set, but the combination of my bedside lamp and the soft glow from my laptop made his eyes gleam.

There was an electricity in the air, one I hadn't sensed before. I knew he felt it too, before he even articulated his next thoughts.

"You're so different than Leila. I mean, I know you've been best friends for, like, ever, but you're really different. You have a much kinder soul than her. You let her take up all the attention and the limelight, but I think you have a really special sparkle of your own by yourself."

"Thanks," I managed, but it was as if my mouth was stuffed with bread or pebbles, like I was trying to breathe underwater. I felt full of a number of emotions—excitement, bashfulness, confusion, and even guilt—even though he hadn't said anything inappropriate to our status as friends.

At least, not yet.

"You're smart and beautiful and kind. You're exciting. There's something about you that I can't believe I've never seen before." Derek seemed almost incredulous but unable to stop himself. He put his hand on my forearm. His fingers lightly traced my skin, and a tingle sent a shock wave straight up my shoulder. "I don't think I've ever truly seen you before."

From his seated position next to me, he put his hands on the sides of my face and kissed me—a hungry kiss, full of curiosity and appreciation and wetness, but also of broken promises and stale coffee and betrayal.

And for a moment of time, I let him. Just one moment.

I came to my senses and pulled away. "We can't do this to her. It's not right."

My voice was barely a whisper, my head full of dance recitals, Girl Scout camping trips, Barbies, sleepovers, and soccer games. No matter what I felt for Derek, whether any of it was real or if it was just a misguided moment in my boyfriend-less existence, he was not mine to kiss. Leila was too important to me, and I was not going to do that to her.

Derek shook himself a little and readjusted. "I understand," he said. "I should probably get going." With a sigh, he ran his hand through his spiky, dirty-blond hair. "It really has been a pleasure working with you."

He was gone, and I had the rest of the night to think about what happened. Derek had started it, but I wasn't blameless. I let it happen, even if only for a moment.

But did we have to tell her? Wouldn't that be worse?

I fell into a fitful sleep, failing to get comfortable or allow my mind to rest. My dreams ranged from good times with Leila to my kiss with Derek, to me trying to explain that it was all a mistake.

At school the next morning, I was determined to find Derek and have an awkward conversation with him. I had always hated conflict, but this problem would fester until we figured out how to handle it. We were mature enough to be able to talk about it—I was confident—and our respective relationships with Leila would certainly withstand one tiny indiscretion.

I would face the music, and I would deal with the anger and disappointment from Leila. But we would get through it together, just as we had with so many petty squabbles over the years, from Leila refusing to admit she borrowed my favorite Barbie without my permission to the time she got me in trouble for copying off my history test. Our friendship had stood the test of time over many other difficulties. It would be tough, but we would get past this too.

And then my life fell apart.

95

CHAPTER

TEN

E ven though Brian was dying to hear about what Betty wrote in code, he acts all frustrated when I tell him my theory.

"It could mean anything. Why bother writing in code if she's still going to be so vague? It might as well have been a grocery list," he mutters. "Why wouldn't she say what she thinks in her diary? Or sketchbook, or whatever. Is she, like, not even being honest with herself?"

I totally get what he is saying but still shrug. Her need for privacy is something I can relate to, for shutting out anyone who wanted to butt into her innermost thoughts. Even though she hasn't written about her relationship with her parents, the fact they didn't even want her things because of her "disgrace" speaks volumes.

"Maybe she was really worried about someone finding out even that? Maybe her parents were really in her business?"

Brian sort of winces at that. Really annoying, invasive parents are better than having no parents at all.

One thing we agree on is that we need more information.

We are back at Abbott Lake a couple of days later when we are both off work, looking for clues. I feel like Scooby Doo should be tagging along with us.

For the hundredth time, I say, "We're not going to find anything. What could we possibly find now anyway?"

Brian shrugs. "Have any better ideas? Plus, it's not like either one of us has much to do today. If nothing else, we'll get some sun and enjoy the peacefulness." He pulls out a large beach towel, unfolds it on the grass, and plops down, adopting the pose of a relaxed teenager versus any type of serious sleuth. Then again, that is what we are—teenagers, not detectives.

He is right, of course, but so am I. All these decades later, it is pretty much impossible to imagine we could find something when the police at the crime scene couldn't. But then I remember something.

"I wonder if they even investigated, though? I mean, they ruled it a suicide, and her parents didn't press it. Do you think they looked for evidence?"

Again, Brian shrugs, but he stares off into the blue sky, thoughtful. "The world's changed so much since then, you know? But I wonder how much it's actually changed right here. The lake's still here after all, and there aren't any buildings around."

Other than the road, which probably wasn't paved back in 1943, things are pretty much the same. We are viewing almost exactly what Betty captured in her sketches. I pull out my phone and search for the pictures I took of her drawings.

Brian scoots closer to see. Despite the fact we are looking on an iPhone, we might as well be back in the 1940s ourselves. Our lake scene is largely unravaged by time.

"The tree looks a little taller," Brian remarks, "unless her perspective was just off. And there's a lot more graffiti on that tree now."

Even with the glare on the phone, we can make out the shapes and shadings she made to capture the markings, natural and man-made, on the bark.

"I don't think that counts as graffiti. They're just carvings. This was probably, like, a lovers' hangout way back." I am aware then of our proximity to each other and back away a little. The shame of the Derek situation is fresh in my mind now that I have released those memories. I flush but point to the detail in the drawing. "See, they were there, even back then."

I enlarge the picture of the tree, but it is too small to make out the specifics. She definitely tried to capture one very large carving near the center.

Brian hoists himself to standing and slow-motion jogs the thirty feet or so to the object of our attention. "Callie, get up." His voice is nearly emotionless. "Check it out."

Always dramatic, this one. I follow his lead anyway.

Up close, the tree is a volume of letters: hearts and initials chiseled in, even a few rude epithets someone bothered to whittle. I greatly prefer the hearts to the bathroom wall-type slander, having been the—unfair—recipient of such disrespect myself.

It seems odd to imagine someone, perhaps decades ago, whiling away the better part of an hour to inscribe something as inane and uninspired as *Cindy G. is a tramp*. How these grooves have endured through the test of time is beyond me. All the winds, rain, and snowfall have failed to erase these messages, both pure and hateful.

I snap a picture of it. Right after my photo of Betty's drawing. I can now flip back and forth between the two.

"Right here—it looks like *B.B. + J.F.* It's right in the heart from the picture." I trace the letters with my finger. "B.B.—Betty Bryson. J.F. must be the father. We just need to figure out who J.F. is. Maybe that's who killed her."

Brian grimaces at me. "Look. It's different from the picture, though. Either Betty or J.F. wasn't into it anymore. Or maybe even someone else didn't want them to be together."

I didn't notice at first, but he is right. The X over the heart is fainter, which kind of doesn't make sense. "But if someone put this X here after the heart, why does it look like it's aged even more? I mean, the initials still look pretty good, and this would've been done later."

"Who knows? Maybe someone else did it. Maybe J.F. was the woodworker but Betty crossed it out after she told him about the baby. Maybe he broke her heart. Or maybe he crossed it out after she died since he was upset? We need to find out who this guy is, though, 'cause I bet that'll tell us something about what happened." His eyes are wide. Brian seems hopeful, and I imagine he expects me to corroborate that this is a good idea.

But I can't. It is not plausible enough.

"Brian, think about what your grandpa said. This didn't happen five or even twenty years ago. This guy's in a nursing home or dead, most likely. He's, like, almost a hundred if he was Betty's age! If he's dead, obviously, we're done with that line of questioning, unless we can get a medium or something."

Brian appears open to that idea. I clarify.

"Kidding! I don't believe in that stuff. And if he's alive, whether or not he had anything to do with it—and whether or not he's the father of the baby—he either won't tell us or doesn't remember. And how are we seriously supposed to find all the age-appropriate guys with the initials J.F. anyway?"

I sit down right by the tree, absentmindedly slapping at a mosquito. It is out early since it isn't quite dusk. I take out my ponytail holder and refashion my hair into a tighter bun, thinking. It is not like we can ignore this information, after all.

Brian sighs and stares out at the lake. He is obviously thinking the same thing.

"High school yearbook?" he says. "Maybe we can get one in the school archives, or maybe your dead great-grandma left one in your aunt's house? My grandpa wouldn't have been in school at the same time, so he's out. And I sure wish we could see the face of the guy in the drawing. It's not like we can compare this dude's back to any yearbook pictures. It looks like he has dark hair, but that's probably more than half of the guys."

It is my turn to shrug. Just one thing gnaws at my mind, and I am almost ashamed to pass it on.

"I don't know how Aunt Evelyn would feel about me asking about Betty. She has some seriously strict ideas about women and morals." I have a mental image of her decked out in Puritan garb, a goodwife. It is Betty, not Hester, who stands at the scaffold, baby clutched to her chest.

Not that Betty ever got that far, though. Her baby was never even able to breathe air into its lungs.

"But what does it matter now to her if Betty's dead? And did they even know each other? Have you said anything to her about the clipping, the sketchbook, or anything?" Brian's exasperation, written plainly on his face, accuses me of being unreasonable. All this happened decades ago, and Aunt Evelyn might be a great source of information.

"If she was eighteen when she died, she's a good decade older than Aunt Evelyn, but that was my great-grandma's age. Maybe they were friends and Aunt Evelyn might have met her if she came to the house. I just need to figure out how to bring it up in a way that won't get her all offended."

"How about if I ask her? I mean, Betty was my relative and all. I'll say that my grandpa was looking through pictures or something and reminiscing about her, and then I'll ask if she remembers her and can share memories." There is that hopeful look again. I can see how much this means to him, even though he is feigning a casual air. He skips a pebble across the shining lake.

"I don't know, Brian. It might even make her more uncomfortable if she has to stifle her reaction around you."

"Callie, you saw how good I am with the elderly. I'm even good with her! I'll change into my preppy clothes and everything."

I laugh at his ridiculous ensemble of Slayer T-shirt, black jeans, and Doc Martens, even on this sweltering summer day. And who is Slayer anyway?

"Dude, you seriously need to embrace the art of soccer shorts and slides." I gesture toward my own super casual outfit.

One of the great things about my friendship with Brian is he doesn't evaluate me based on my appearance. There is no need to choose the right clothes or put on makeup. He doesn't make me feel like I have to put on a show. In Cagney, even if I am just getting together with a female friend, I always obsess over my outfit, shoes, jewelry, and makeup. Now, I throw on whatever and feel comfortable looking like myself.

I have to admit, though, I have noticed that Brian's clothes have become somewhat less severe as the summer moves on. He is still wearing the ear gauges, of course. I think he would need a plastic surgeon to get rid of those. But he had added the tiniest bit of color into his wardrobe, and I swear, some of his jeans come from Old Navy rather than Hot Topic.

Maybe he has noticed that he doesn't need to pretend to be someone else around me either, so whatever his Emo or Goth look was before has been massively toned down. Perhaps he is just dressing like himself again.

We haven't talked about how close we have become. Brian and I aren't mushy like that. But I think we both know that we are close, and we both appreciate how good it is to have a real friend.

Still, I deliver my parting shot: "Even Poe would be wearing a tank top by now."

We pack up our stuff. I think he is pissed off at me until I hear him croak out, "Nevermore," before getting back into the truck.

Lake of Secrets

CHAPTER

ELEVEN

July Fourth comes and goes like any other day, without any fireworks or barbecues. I am so wrapped up thinking about Betty that I barely even wonder what celebrations my friends and family are attending in Cagney.

Aunt Evelyn doesn't like surprises, so I don't spring Brian's visit on her right away despite how anxious we are to forage any crumbs of truth about J.F. I prep her in advance by checking if it is okay for Brian to ask her some questions about her memories as a teen. She seems agreeable enough, so we have settled on a day for him to come over.

With J.F. on my mind, it is tough not to sneak some glances at the names of male residents when I call out their dietary requirements to my coworker behind the counter. After all, some of the oldest men are in the same age group. As a dietary aide, of course, I don't have access to any roster of patients, but as luck would have it that day, I have been assigned to be the food caller.

I only have enough time to speed read each resident's name,

though, since I need to concentrate on what their meals are. As much as I want more information about J.F., I don't want to screw up and give anyone the wrong food. But during my always-hectic shift, the only J.F. is a Joan Fitzgerald, who biology tells me cannot be the father of anyone's baby.

Even though it is only Brian, Aunt Evelyn is unaccustomed to company, so she has been bustling around, getting ready for his visit. She doesn't bake, but she has emptied a package of homemade-looking chocolate chip cookies into a ceramic cat-printed tray, which matches the pitcher of iced tea sweating on the coffee table. We sit in the living room, Aunt Evelyn's only real seating area, but the TV is resting for once.

Brian seems comfortable enough in his preppy uniform. I imagine him getting ready and combing his hair the way he imagines a "nice young man" should look, though he has still covered up his scar. He plays his part well, which isn't surprising. It is probably genuine, with edgy, alternative Brian being more a disguise.

We sit around, smiling at each other awkwardly, for a few minutes, eating cookies and drinking the sickeningly sweet tea. I catch Brian stifling a wince after the first sip, but he grins and bears it. This guy will stop at nothing for intel.

He finally clears his throat. "Ms. Reynolds, I was hoping I could ask you some questions about a relative of mine whom you may have known when you were young."

He is obviously a little nervous. While he is probably more comfortable speaking with old folks than about ninety-nine percent of teenagers, he is not just after donations this time. Brian is playing his cards carefully, or maybe it is Jenga: Brian wants to surge forward since he won't get anywhere otherwise, but he is worried that everything could topple down if he is too forceful.

Tthose big brown eyes, so open and sincere, must have the intended effect. Aunt Evelyn nods her head for him to continue.

"She was my grandfather's cousin. Her name was Betty Bryson."

Thankfully, Aunt Evelyn remains docile and refrains from

breaking into some sort of spitting tirade about girls who are soiled or something like that.

"Yes, Brian. Of course. I knew Betty. It's so sad what happened to her."

"Were you friends? How well did you know her? My grandpa's been thinking about her lately and told me some of the story. But he was a little kid back then and wasn't really aware of, you know, some factors in the situation." It is not every day he talks to a lady in her late eighties about teen pregnancy, after all.

She fingers her necklace and adopts the glassy-eyed look I have seen so often in her and residents in the nursing home, the one where it seems like they are looking in the past. Aunt Evelyn is speaking to us, the people right in front of her, but I don't think she is seeing us anymore. She may as well have been envisioning a scene from her youth.

"Betty and Lillian, my sister and Callie's great-grandmother, were close friends. My sister and I had a big gap in between us—the middle child having died before I was even born—and that made us closer. She never minded including her little sister, so I got to know Betty quite well. There we are, in that photo."

Aunt Evelyn smiles faintly and points to the picture I noticed on my first day here, the one of the three girls wearing plaid skirts.

All this time, then, this whole summer, Betty has been watching over me while I have suffered through endless hours of television. Here she was, hanging on the wall, before I even found the newspaper article or met her distant relative. I knew her photo seemed familiar to me, and this is why: I had seen her before.

"Was Lillian still friends with her when she died?" Brian asks. "And do you think Betty wanted to die?"

Aunt Evelyn shakes her head and casts down her eyes. "Lillian and Betty grew apart during their senior year of high school, I'm afraid, and she stopped coming around the house. I really didn't know much about her at the time of her death. It was still shocking, of course. Lillian took it especially hard."

I wait for her to tell us more, such as why they stopped being friends. She remains pensive, sipping her sweet tea.

"Did people really think she killed herself?" I ask. "Do you remember what everyone was saying after they found her?"

She sighs, a wispy sound in the quiet room. "Brian, I think it's best your grandfather was so young at the time. It's good he doesn't remember. I dare not speak ill of the dead."

"Please. Please tell me so my grandfather can have some peace."

"As you wish." Another maddeningly slow sip. "No one told me at the time. I was so young. But the rumors found their way to me eventually. She was with child, Brian. It was common for girls back then to marry young and bear children, even still in high school, as so many of their beaus were rushing off to war. But Betty hadn't married." Sip.

As painful as it is listening to this slow spilling of information, it seems as excruciating for her to tell us. This tidbit isn't news to either of us, but by tacit agreement, we don't tell Aunt Evelyn that we have already found out some things about both Betty's life and death.

"Many believed Betty ended her life due to the shame she would bring on her family. Her parents were honest, respectable, God-fearing people who never deserved such a disgrace. Perhaps it was her attempt at kindness to them. Sadly, everyone found out about the pregnancy anyway."

"It seems far sadder to me that she died than that anyone found out about the pregnancy," I mumble, trying to keep the bitterness out of my tone. "Do you know who the father was?"

A hint of her disapproval comes out when she answers. "I don't care to gossip now, nor did I back then. No, I do not."

Brian obviously wants to ask about J.F., but that would entail giving Aunt Evelyn more information about our digging, and it is clear she doesn't approve of the subject. I know I am right when she begins busying herself by clearing our dishes.

He holds himself back but not entirely. "Do you have any other pictures of her? I bet my grandpa would love to see them. Or maybe a yearbook where I could find out things she liked to do? Did Lillian leave her yearbook here when she moved away?"

"Dear boy, let your grandfather keep his happy memories of his cousin. Nothing happy will come from drudging up the details of her indiscretions." With that, Aunt Evelyn walks the few steps into her modest kitchen.

The conversation is officially over.

CHAPTER

TWELVE

Brian and I meet at his house the next day since he has Wi-Fi. It was one of the non-negotiables for him when he moved in with his grandpa after he lost his parents, and now the formerly internet-shy Mr. Spencer enjoys surfing the web almost as much as any teenager. I brought my laptop so we can double our efforts.

"So, how are you with research?" I ask Brian after we get set up at the big kitchen table.

Mr. Spencer is at work. Brian hasn't mentioned if he has been upfront about our little "investigation" of Betty, but I have a feeling it could be a sore subject after that initial clash I witnessed while looking at the contents of Betty's shoebox.

"I got an A on my last research paper. Does that count? Not so sure how I'll do with this."

We don't have much of a plan, so it is not shocking when we come up with nothing. A Google search returns a surprising number of Betty Brysons, both living and dead, but none are the right Betty.

"Let's try a search for men with the initials J.F.," I suggest, but this is equally useless.

First, I only find celebrities, and I get nothing at all relevant once I add in "Deerville, PA." There are a few services offered where I can pay $19.95 for access, but I am not willing to buck up when it looks like that only gives addresses and telephone numbers.

Next, I try to find digitized newspapers from back in those days to see if Betty's name showed up anywhere besides the article about her death. Thinking I am on to something, I type in *"Deerville Daily,"* the name of the local newspaper, which comes out weekly—in direct contrast with its title. I am directed to a new search of *"Deerville Daily* back issues digital." This leads me to nothing, though. It seems I can only view the front page of some random issues, and even these come out fuzzy and, therefore, illegible.

My unwieldy "How can I find information on people who lived in Deerville PA in 1943" query takes me to the historical society's website, and I get excited again for a moment. I navigate the tabs to find a photograph collection, then type in "1943" to see what happens, if maybe I can browse pictures and find Betty cozied up to someone. However, it seems I can only view a description of the photographs and not the pictures themselves.

I would have to fill out a request form, which seems silly since I don't even know what I am asking for. Under the "history" tab, I read about an informational section in the local library. Maybe we will have more luck if we can physically access this information?

That thought feels foreign, growing up in the age of technology, but I am not getting anywhere through the regular internet search tactics I am familiar with.

Based on Brian's puckered brow, he hasn't made much progress either. He confirms this with a frustrated shake of his head and the downward tilt to his lips.

"Time to get some professional help," I say. "Let's go to the library."

Lake of Secrets

As it turns out, Brian has to get to work, but I am anxious to see what I can find and decide to go by myself. Deerville Public Library is only a few minutes away from Briar Creek Manor. It is a shame I didn't know about it in my early days in Deerville, when I was at the mercy of Aunt Evelyn's deafening TV set for my only entertainment.

Like many structures in town, it is a charming old building, one that has been able to age gracefully with obvious caretaking. Though I doubt the budget from the town is large, somehow, the gilded letters gleam, the blond bricks are clean and shiny, and the landscaping appears cheerful. White and purple hydrangeas decorate the fresh mulch. Even before the automatic doors admit me, I feel invited in.

I have always loved a library: the cover and anonymity offered by a darkened corner where rows of bookcases intersect, the golden silence you can find when the rest of the world seems to be yelling into cellphones. Maybe it is genetic.

My mom told me she had worked in the library in college. She said there was tremendous peace inside the dim cubicles while she filled in the ledgers for her accounting homework, sheltered from the chaos of dorm life. Part of her job involved shelf reading: checking that books were in the right place. While she has always been a supreme rule follower, she couldn't help but get distracted when she came upon a particularly interesting book she wouldn't have ordinarily found—a slim volume of African mythology or a pictorial how-to guide on origami.

Libraries can be full of hidden treasures, even in those due date cards they used to stamp when you signed out books, before everything went digital. My mom explained it to me when I asked long ago.

As a child, when I had far more time on my hands to visit a library and come home with the maximum allowance of books, I would look at the dates and imagine what someone was doing on August 9, 1968, when the book was due, whether they returned it on time. It used to fascinate me to see how a book I checked out had been unread for as long as twenty years. Once the digital system arrived, though, you never knew when a book was last loved.

Which is why it is crazy I haven't visited this place before—I have become one of the many to leave these books untouched, unappreciated.

An arctic blast of air conditioning slaps me in the face. If I were coming straight from the sauna of Aunt Evelyn's house, this would feel like a welcome refuge, but Mr. Spencer actually had air conditioning installed into his old home, so I have no need of cooling down.

I take in the colorful summer reading posters, the ads for upcoming library events, and the hushes from parents attempting to control excited children discovering new books to take home. While I have never been one to endure shrieks from kids, I can appreciate a child who chooses a book over an iPad.

It is a bad habit of mine to waste copious amounts of time figuring things out on my own rather than asking for help from a trained professional, but I have already tried and failed finding information enough for one day. Since I need to report to work later, there is only so much time to spare.

The lady at the front desk—maybe a librarian, maybe a clerk or something—appears sufficiently out of place for Deerville, with her bejeweled cat-eye glasses, polka dot dress, sleek bob, and full tattoo sleeve. She is like a cross between a 1950s housewife and a biker, and the effect is pretty cool.

Although she seems nearly my mom's age, she is far from the Ann Taylor/White House Black Market business casual type I think of as "mom chic," yet she has clearly taken great care with her appearance. Somehow, though, she fits in just fine in a library, surrounded by books, and I feel like she won't judge me for being weird when I tell her what I am looking for.

I introduce myself and give her a quick but edited overview: I am looking for information about a girl who died in 1943, and I have read the article on her death, but I have not seen anything else. It doesn't seem necessary to get into the whole side story of having a box of her possessions, and I am not sure Mr. Spencer would approve of me sharing that with a stranger.

"Anything in particular you're hoping to find?" She smiles, making me wonder if I should start wearing red lipstick. It is so glamourous. "I'm a local yokel, but the name's not familiar, which is surprising. People generally stay here forever and keep having babies." She rolls her eyes dramatically.

Maybe I can get a little extra insight if I pique her curiosity, yet I still want to guard some of the private information I have learned about Betty. "Anything about her life or death. She was a relative of my friend, and he's trying to find out information."

This sounds a little lame. Her perfectly groomed eyebrows raise, almost asking, "Oh, a *friend*?"

I sense the faint flush coming into my face. "It's sort of a historical investigation we're doing."

Janice smirks and introduces herself. She is not only a reference librarian, but a member of the DAR, which she explains stands for Daughters of the American Revolution. It is a group which preserves heritage and is descended from patriots of the Revolutionary War. She then gives me a tour of the local history section of the library.

"The first place I tell people to check if they have a name and date range, which you do, is the newspaper index. It's like a shortcut...since old newspapers, especially the non-digitized ones, aren't searchable like a PDF or Word document or something."

She points me to a bookcase full of hardbound volumes, like the ancient encyclopedia set my paternal grandfather has moldering away in his study.

After a quick search, Janice pulls out a medium-sized book. "1938 to 1943. That should be a good start to see if she's listed in the local newspaper anywhere besides when she died. I'm going to assume that, if she was only eighteen at the time of death, not too much newspaper-worthy stuff happened before then." She opens the volume and starts paging through the long lists of names, listed alphabetically, to the B section.

Some names have a single entry while others have several. It is kind of surreal to see how some people are listed for all—or, at least, all who go to the library and look at this record—to see. Information appears in columns, classified into categories such as birth, marriage, death, divorce, or crime.

"Can you believe that someone actually went through all the papers for years and years and sorted out this information?" When I shake my head in disbelief, showing that I think it must be an arduous and thankless task, she hits me with, "Believe it, sister. Being a librarian/historian isn't all story hour for toddlers and checking out books." She looks pensive for a moment, and says, "That can be a pain in the butt too, to be fair."

We find Betty's name. She is indexed in a couple of other places besides her death notice, July 20, 1943. Each listing has only a short phrase to describe it: The first, in May, is a mention of scholarship recipients, and the second is a picture of her from June of that year, just over a month before she died, as part of the graduating class. There are no other mentions.

It is sad that the only accomplishments the newspaper found noteworthy of Betty's short life occurred so close to her death. There is not even an obituary. The article I have already read about her death was Betty's final mention.

There is no need for me to look up that one, of course, but I want to read the articles with her other mentions. The index gives the exact date when the paper came out, so Janice walks over to a metal cabinet, scans some labels, and pulls out a small box. I thought we would be looking at old newspapers in scrapbooks or something.

Maybe I am making a bizarre face because she says, "It's microfilm. Ever heard of it?"

"I think so? I haven't used it, though."

Janice walks me over to an old-fashioned machine with a big screen, but it doesn't appear to be a computer. There is no keyboard or tower. It appears to be like a hybrid computer/sewing machine/ microscope with knobs, gears, glass plates, and lenses.

She unrolls a few inches from the spool of film on a canister, like the non-digital film I had to use in photography class. It is kind of like loading a camera, placing the film through these different parts, and sliding the apparatus back under the lens once it is wound through. After Janice flicks a switch on the side, the screen illuminates, projecting a fairly clear, sepia-tinted newspaper image. She shows me how to use the various knobs and gears to focus it more and advance the film.

"I'll leave you to it." Janice seems to enjoy the incredulous expression that must be on my face while I gain insight into the past. "Let me know if you need help with the second spool."

I am transported back in time with the *Deerville Daily*, noticing national headlines on the front page—"Tunis and Bizerte Liberated by Allied Troops." I don't know who the heck they are, but it is obviously war-related—and small-town news in the pages which follow.

Most of it seems pretty boring: school board meetings, a front-page article about a cow that won a prize at the local fair, and most peculiarly, a section listing residents' most mundane activities. I don't know how "Mr. and Mrs. Ronald Thompson visited their daughter, Mrs. Henry Mitchell, in New York last week" and "Mr. and Mrs. William Blakely are keeping house for Mr. Charles Anderson during his wife's sickness" count as newsworthy, but here I am, reading it, amused by its very dullness.

Although it only comes out once a week, the newspaper is still small, at only eight pages an issue, in large contrast with my dad's thick *Wall Street Journal* he reads every day. But the staff has used the space efficiently, cramming in not just the news, but advertisements of all sorts. I skim these while I advance the film to page six, where the index tells me I will find notice of Betty.

This method clearly isn't as direct as the Control+F one I use in a Word document, but it is easy enough to find information and extremely entertaining to peruse the paper. From the market hawking six-cent boxes of cornflakes to the individual saying he would like to buy your old, worn-out horse for fox food, I can't help thinking how much times have changed.

And then I find what I came for, even if it is not much—an article titled "Deerville High Scholarship Recipients." It provides only a short paragraph on each winner, but it is still enlightening.

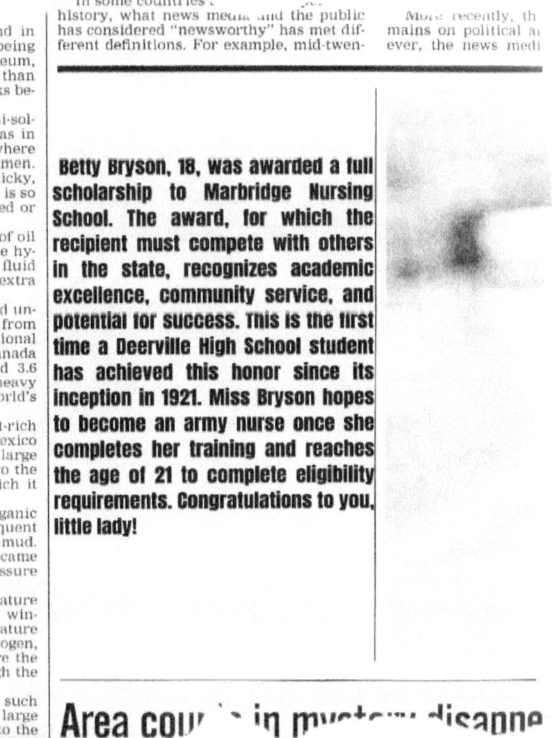

Betty Bryson, 18, was awarded a full scholarship to Marbridge Nursing School. The award, for which the recipient must compete with others in the state, recognizes academic excellence, community service, and potential for success. This is the first time a Deerville High School student has achieved this honor since its inception in 1921. Miss Bryson hopes to become an army nurse once she completes her training and reaches the age of 21 to complete eligibility requirements. Congratulations to you, little lady!

Huh. I'll skip over the blatant sexism of "little lady" and get right to the bigger issue. She is Deervilles's poster child for success in May but doesn't even get a proper obituary when she dies a mere two months later?

As depicted in the June newspaper, Betty's achievements are equally impressive. Although it is only a picture of several graduating seniors in their caps and gowns, only two have been named in the photo's caption: a young man listed as the valedictorian and Betty Bryson, salutatorian. Wow.

Betty was no fickle girl who would have given up at a sign of conflict. She was an ambitious, diligent, community-oriented person who would have figured something out.

The library comes through where Aunt Evelyn did not. Janice shows me the yearbooks next. It is just a slim, hardbound book with a cracked spine, probably a quarter of the size of the ridiculously expensive, metal-embossed ones Cagney High manufactures and manipulates me—well, my parents—into buying every year. The effect of war is ever-present, from the American flag decorations to the tributes to both students and faculty who have left Deerville High for the military. I am looking for two things: more on Betty herself and possibilities of who J.F. might have been.

Based on what I already know about Betty, her list of activities fails to surprise me, and neither does the photo. It is the same one Mr. Spencer has. Betty's blurb identifies her in the academic track—versus general or commercial, whatever that means—and lists her activities to include National Honor Society, yearbook committee, glee club, book club, and community service.

All that potential and passion, just to be snuffed out so soon and forgotten. It just about makes me sick.

Next, I start looking for J.F. I find a light-haired Joseph Freed, who I am pretty sure I can dismiss because of Betty's sketch by the lake, and a handsome, dark-haired Jack Fegley, whose activities, amongst others, also include National Honor Society and community service.

Interesting.

So, they definitely knew each other. Of that I am certain, though it doesn't prove he was the father and/or the killer. But he *is* a dark-haired J.F. who was at least an acquaintance.

Unlike my own high school yearbooks, only seniors are shown.

The underclassmen may as well have been invisible. The yearbook moves from pictures of the seniors to those of the mostly grim-faced faculty. Then it is all club activity pictures, some candids, a few ads or congratulatory notices, and a few short poems.

Jackpot.

And I think it is a love poem, even though it is a bit gruesome and depressing. Poetry is not really my thing, but Betty liked to be cryptic.

My blue jay flies too low to the ground,
Risking his freedom, scorching his wings.
He can soar high until he is bound
By duty or love; he sweetly sings.
If I give my heart, there's more to lose,
Since my assent has consequences.
At the end I don't know what to choose:
Burning bridges, or mending fences?
Roots link me to land, wrought to a grave
Do what you must; it's he whom I'll save.

-Betty Bryson, Class of '43

I make a quick mental note of her rhyme scheme—ABABCD-CDEE—and consistent syllable count, though I don't think there is a name for that specific pattern since she stopped short of a traditional sonnet. Now it is time to analyze. I have had plenty of practice in English class over the years.

First, is the "blue jay flies." A reference to J.F.? Whether or not the first-person speaker is Betty herself, it is obvious that the blue jay is a metaphor for the speaker's lover. She is torn between being with him versus letting him go, and there is something holding them back from being together. The speaker thinks he may become hurt in some way if he stays with her or that someone else would be hurt. She would rather endure the pain herself than allow this.

Could this refer to her coded message, the "freedom" and "duty" parts? Was J.F. already with a serious girlfriend when he turned his head for Betty? Does the "grave" part represent the death of their love? I wonder how Betty would evaluate my interpretation, especially after reading her reactions to various novels she read.

How many people took note of the poem after Betty's body was found? Did the police read it and see it as some sort of suicide note, due to the "wrought to a grave" part? I don't interpret it that way at all; I think she wrote it before she ultimately decided to be with him, before she became pregnant with the baby. After all, Betty couldn't have been very far along in her pregnancy when she was found or else she would have been showing. The yearbook material would have needed to be submitted well in advance, for printing purposes.

I need to find out more about this Jack Fegley to see if he is a possibility, even though I know he is not the only one. These are just the boys she graduated with. J.F. could be anyone: a boy from a different graduating class, someone from a different school, even someone older. But my time is up.

After gathering up the notes I scribbled down, I thank Janice for all her help and walk back to the car, my head full of the poem, awards, and the tremendous loss that Betty's life really is.

Lake of Secrets

CHAPTER

THIRTEEN

At work a couple of days later, I am pouring tea and coffee, hooking Mr. Danvers up with his Sweet'N Low, when a sharp gasp comes from one of the residents.

With Sally Kraemer's still-slender figure, fine white hair pinned and curled on each side of her head in an old-fashioned style, and bright red lipstick, she is like an ancient version of the beautiful young woman she must have once been. Unlike many of her peers, who go for the standard old lady uniform of shapeless cat-themed shirt with elastic-waisted pants, she wears a fashionable, albeit vintage-looking, red dress. Despite her strange formality, she appears elegant. It is clear she exerts a great effort into getting ready for dinner.

I don't know her and haven't served her before. She is new as of this week, but I head over to see if I should call for a nurse.

"It's you." A strange look on her face—she must be one of the many who gets stuck in the past. I open my mouth to tell her my name, but she says, "Betty?"

Though Betty is constantly on my mind, the name is popular in the nursing home. I don't think anything of it.

"Betty Bryson? How are you here?" Her delicate, blue-veined but carefully manicured hand reaches for my wrist, which I reflexively pull back.

My blood runs cold. Someone who not only knew her, but, like Brian and Mr. Spencer, thinks I resemble her in some way. What are the chances that I was the one who found the article on Betty's death? It is a crazy and almost spooky series of coincidences.

"I'm Callie. I work here. I'm not Betty," I say, trying to keep the tremor from my voice.

"But you died. I know you died. And you were in the family way!" She raises her finger and points at me.

I am not Betty, and I am definitely *not* pregnant, but my cheeks flush with mortification anyway. Before I can think better of it, before she attracts any more attention, before she snaps back to the present, I ask quietly, "Who killed me, then? And who was the father of my baby?"

"Tramp. You killed yourself and your bastard child too. I know what you did." Mrs. Kraemer no longer appears beautiful to me. Her hate and cruelty have turned her ugly, a stain no amount of red lipstick or fancy hairstyle can cover.

Her shrill voice has caught the attention of an orderly from the hall—a broad, forty-ish man with tattoos all up and down his arms. He looks like the right guy to call when there's a problem.

"Everything okay?" he asks. He knows the drill. Sometimes, the residents get upset. I just hope he didn't hear everything she said to me.

"Yes. She thought I was someone else." Hot tears prick my eyes but, thankfully, stay at bay. I don't know this orderly, but I also don't want him to see me cry, especially when it would seem like such an inappropriate reaction.

While I finish my tables, I don't stop to chat like I normally do. When I take my fifteen-minute break early, I head outside for some solitude.

Maybe I feel bad for the disrespect to Betty. After all, she seems so real to me now that I have read her words, seen her photographs and sketches, and even dreamt about her. But it is also a painful reminder about my last couple of months of school.

I wasn't ever the one who caused conflict in my relationship with Leila. In fact, there were times she caused so much drama between the two of us I would purposely keep my distance, thinking I would rather have fewer friends than deal with her—the grenade waiting to explode. We would enjoy a fun sleepover at her house, staying up late, eating pizza, and playing video games on a Friday night, but then I would sit next to her at Sunday school, and she would act like she didn't even know me.

It was always like that. Leila was hot and cold. When the sun shines, you bask in and savor its light and warmth, but it won't come out from the clouds to comfort you when it is cold and dark. That was Leila.

It took me until around sixth grade to work up the nerve to blow her off. The thing with Leila was, she didn't show everyone her true self. Teachers loved her. She could do no wrong, like when she broke the teacher's coffee mug and someone else ended up getting in trouble. And maybe I was a stronger soccer player on the field than she was, yet she started as striker while I warmed the bench. People just took to her. Was I jealous? Maybe a little sometimes, but it never was really about that for me.

Should I have taken it as a compliment that she didn't wear a mask around me? It didn't feel like any sort of prize, that is for sure. How could she act nice and friendly with strangers when she treated me like I was beneath her? Sometimes, I would feel like we were having fun, and then the other people would leave, and she would start taunting me, telling me that I embarrassed her by laughing too loudly or wearing the wrong color shirt, or something equally inane.

But when I tried to pull away, there she was, telling me how sad she was that we "drifted apart," that she wanted nothing more than for us to be close again. Inevitably, I bought into her charm and let myself get pulled back into her vortex.

So, it shouldn't have come as a surprise, I guess, what she did that day.

I wouldn't say that I am a superstitious person, but it was sort of like I had a premonition as soon as I walked through the double doors into school that fateful morning. Maybe I was feeling guilty and experiencing the usual anxiety I get whenever I have to leave my comfort zone. I was a woman on a mission; I had to find Derek before he spilled the beans to Leila.

Did I actually hear anyone talking about me? It was probably my imagination. No one ever seemed to care what Callie Quinn was up to since I was so vanilla. There were no skeletons in my closet—I must have been one of only a handful of girls to make it into junior year of high school without a stain on my reputation.

Still, I sort of knew before I saw her, before I saw them.

She was waiting for me at my locker.

Obviously, Leila knew what had happened. I could see it in her cold, hard smirk. And I realized what was coming before she said it, but it still felt like a slap to my face, a knife to my heart. That sounds exaggerated, but I physically experienced my feelings of dread.

"Bitch." She almost spat or growled it, the word so low and guttural that it could have been mistaken for a grunt. But I knew Leila. I understood how she operated.

But I don't know what I would have said if I had gotten the chance to talk. I opened my mouth to say something, but my voice fell silent. She continued.

"Poor little Callie. Everyone just feels so bad for you, you know?" Her voice had taken on that mocking, singsong quality it got when she was worked up. I had heard it many times over the years. Sometimes, it had been used to protect me from someone else, like in second grade, when Sonia Cartwright told everyone I was a boy.

I had never even talked to Sonia before. To this day, I don't know what possessed her to say that about me. I mean, I had long hair and even went through a phase where I wore dresses every day. But what I remember most is the relief that Leila was there to defend me.

Sonia was the one who ended up in tears that day, not me, all because of Leila, my defender. But now Leila was thrusting her evil power onto me.

"I can't tell you how many times I've heard people ask why I'm friends with you," she said, her voice rising dramatically. She was gaining an audience. "They're like, 'Leila, why do you hang out with that sad, boring, geek? Has she ever even had a boyfriend?' And then I'm like, 'I don't even know if she likes boys. She's into, like, books and movies and stuff, but I feel bad for her, you know?'"

As much as I was boiling inside, I felt disappointed in Leila for how she showcased herself as a ditz. Leila read almost as much as I did. But this was only one of many things on my mind while my face flamed. I tried to make myself smaller and smaller, wanting to disappear. She hurled forth these harmful thoughts like spears at my naked, vulnerable self.

"So I tell everyone that you're, like, my charity case. I feel good about myself for being a friend to you. It's, like, my civic duty or something." Her voice continued to rise, and the crowd gathered. I thought it was for show, but then she looked me straight in the eyes, and I saw her wrath. "All those years...All those years of letting you tag along with me...I could have shut you out, like everyone else did, but I let you in. *You*, Callie, the freaking weirdo."

She kept talking. Her soliloquy was reaching its crescendo and would only get worse as each insult hit its mark. I focused on trying to breathe, but everything started blurring around me. Tears filled my eyes.

People actually laughed at me, snickering away like this was a comedy show. Did they really even know if I had done anything wrong? Did they even know about the betrayal yet, or were they just cruising along in Leila's sunlight, happy to burn through anything that came into its path?

"But meanwhile, my charity case sets her sights on my boyfriend, of all people. The bitch stakes her claim on what is mine."

Her voice seemed to echo. What felt like the entire student body hung on every word. And I felt so guilty, so very ashamed of what I had done, even though I didn't initiate it and only responded for the briefest second. I was going to tell her, was going to make it right...

"He told me, Callie. Derek told me what you did to him, and let me tell you, honey..." She rolled the word, a grotesque parody of the term of endearment it is supposed to be. "You will be very, very sorry." She tapped my nose three times, punctuating each of her last words. Her sparkling nail polish caused a glitter tornado in front of my eyes.

She turned away triumphantly. I sat down on the floor by my

locker and cried into my arms while the students around me, people I had thought were friends, laughed and whispered openly about me—the social pariah I had suddenly become.

And from that moment on, I was ruined. I never got to explain myself to her because she wouldn't let me. If I even got near her, Leila started making a spectacle of me. The hot, angry tears constantly threatened to spill from my eyes.

She would wait for them to come so she could say, "Stop embarrassing yourself, Callie."

There she would be, holding hands with Derek, who was even guiltier than I was. Maybe the look in his eyes when he quickly stole a glance at me was compassion or guilt, or even a silent threat not to tell the truth. I didn't even know.

The weeks passed, but things didn't improve. Soccer became a nightmare. I had thought those girls were my friends too, but I was getting balls purposely kicked at my head when I turned away. People either ignored me or made rude comments, and I ended up getting kicked or knocked over during each scrimmage.

Anytime it happened, Leila stood there, leering at me.

Coach begged me to stay and tried to get me to tell him what the problem was. I didn't want to, but I quit. Of course, I had to delete my TikTok, Instagram, and Facebook accounts. It was too much to bear: the inappropriate pictures and videos posted to my timeline that my parents and relatives could have seen; the messages from boys I barely knew, offering their "services."

I withdrew more into my mind, wanting to be invisible. Rather than stand up for myself, feeling it was useless, I would just walk away if anyone started talking about me.

I skipped first period a few times because that was World Cultures class, which I had with both Leila and Derek. Though I was still doing all my work, the stupid teacher called my mom anyway. Before I knew it, I was missing one of my Leila-free classes because I had been called to the guidance counselor's office.

It was all just so claustrophobic to be stuck in disgusting Mr. Thompson's cheesy broom closet of a workspace, with its fake motivational quotes and kitten poster no self-respecting adult male should have. My mom and Mr. Thompson just stared at me, waiting for me to spill my secrets because I had never skipped any classes before.

A vault. I said nothing. And I didn't make any excuses, although the thought crossed my mind. I just said that sometimes I didn't want to go to that class.

"You know, Callie, Mr. Summerfield didn't even write you up for skipping. He thought it was more important to work through your troubles," Mr. Thompson said.

I could sense his sweaty, beefy arm wanting to push the box of tissues toward me to open the floodgates. Perhaps I was supposed to feel happy that my teacher and guidance counselor had spared me from a detention, but I would honestly rather have stayed in the cafeteria after school with a book instead of here being grilled.

Mom sat there with a look of concern on her face, twisting her engagement and wedding rings around. But she really didn't say much unless directly addressed by Mr. Thompson. I couldn't read her, and they couldn't read me.

On the ride home, she asked me if there was anything she should know about.

"No, Mom," I responded. "There's really nothing. I'm not on drugs, and I'll not skip that class anymore." I left it at that and stared out the window, expressionless.

She asked if I wanted to go to Panera Bread for dinner and acted as if the whole thing had never happened. When the prom rolled around and I didn't go, she said nothing, except that maybe I could wear the dress I had bought next year. She allowed me to live in the fictional world where everything was fine and things were normal, just like before.

By the time school ended and she threw her plan at me about going to Aunt Evelyn's for the summer, she had created a whole fictional life for me, where I was the same girl I had always been. She lay the foundation for me to act like I was going to miss out on what would have been a super fun summer with friends, when really, I would be escaping a life that had become completely unbearable.

And I went along with it, acting like I still had friends and happiness in my life.

After a little while, I kind of started believing it.

This supposed summer of torture is an opportunity for me to find a way back to myself.

In the beginning of the summer, I blamed my former friends' lack of contact with me on busy schedules and poor cellphone reception, when really, everyone had stopped being friends with me. It was just easier to let myself go along with Mom's fiction. Everything was fine. I was fine—a normal teenager who didn't want her parents controlling her life.

I wasn't fine.

Maybe my parents were in denial that something was wrong with me. Perhaps they should have said something about the horrible things they saw posted to Facebook. I mean, my mom is always checking it. Maybe they searched my room for drugs and alcohol— of which they would have found none—when I was at school and did a great job of covering their tracks.

Should they have forced me to see a therapist? Was it painfully obvious that I needed help in some way?

If I was wearing rose-colored glasses before, I have taken them off now. I can see everything for what it is, even if what I see is pretty freaking bleak.

But actually, I feel okay now.

I am not sad or depressed about how things went down, and I am no longer in denial about losing the life and friends I once had. But I am not going to be a victim or throw myself a pity party. I won't let Leila or anyone else be the judge of me.

131

CHAPTER

FOURTEEN

Brian stares at me in disbelief from across the dregs of his mocha latte at Nan's. I finish telling him about Mrs. Kraemer...and the other stuff I had to get off my chest.

"Well?" I need him to say something. He is my only real friend at the moment. Now that I am being honest with myself, I am scared he will reject me for bending the truth.

As much as I want to feel lighter for verbalizing what I went through, the anxiety of even more alienation hangs above me—a black, heavy mass in the otherwise cheerful coffee shop. After all, he has been straight with me about the darkness he has experienced, yet I acted like everything was fine with me.

"What do you think?"

The inappropriately perky "Mr. Sandman" plays on the jukebox, conflicting with the turmoil of my emotions. I break off a tiny piece of my gigantic black-and-white cookie, but it is strangely unappealing to me right now.

Say something.

I crumble it into pieces between my thumb and pointer fingers, unable to meet his eyes.

But he finds mine anyway, and they look sad rather than angry.

"I'm just...I don't know...really surprised. I thought you left behind a pretty great life at home, so it is kind of unnerving, you know? It sounds really, really awful, and you didn't even talk to anyone about it. Did you ever think that you should tell your parents or maybe a therapist, or somebody? I just feel bad for you."

"I don't need you to pity me," I say in a small voice, kind of embarrassed about everything. But it is a tremendous relief that the story is finally out of me, even though it took me a few more days to process it all after the memories flooded in. "I really didn't want to talk to anyone. I wanted things to just be normal again. I guess I was lying to myself to try to make myself feel better."

My eyes are dangerously close to leaking, but I blink a few times and clear them.

"But like I said, I gave it a lot of thought today when that situation with Mrs. Kraemer happened—which was beyond weird, by the way—and I feel ready to move on and not let Leila or anyone else have that control over me, you know?"

I am talking too much and too fast, so I take a sip of my now room temperature cappuccino to slow down. After gulping the disappointing concoction, I force a smile.

"I'm okay, Brian. I get it that I wasn't for a while, but my time here has been good for me. Aunt Evelyn and you have been good for me. I just didn't know if you'd be weird about it or mad at me that I didn't give you the real deal, you know?"

He nods. "Hey, I get that reality can be hard, and I'm glad you felt like you could be honest with me and tell your story." He reaches across the table, past my mutilated cookie, and places his hand on mine just for a moment. "You've been good for me too. In case you haven't noticed, my social life has gotten a whole lot better since you moved here. I wasn't exactly tearing it up in the friend department. Let's be misfits together. Mystery-solving misfits! Let's figure out Betty's story since she never got the chance to tell it herself."

He proceeds to fill me in about following up on the Jack Fegley lead. Not to take away all his fun and mindful of the fact I had actual responsibilities outside of my sleuthing life, I had already shared my information, showed him my notes, and sent him to Janice.

While I am sure he also received the raised-eyebrow treatment, he doesn't mention it.

"So, it doesn't look like this Jack's the guy, either for the father or the killer. I mean, he became a priest, and they're not supposed to, you know, get girls pregnant. And he did all these good things for the community." He rattles off a few, and I have to admit, Jack sounds pretty saint-like.

"Maybe that was her quandary, though? They loved each other, but he was going to be a priest, and she didn't want to ruin that life for him by getting in the way?" I recall the line in the poem about saving him and the crucifix around her neck in her senior portrait. Could he have given that to her? Or could that show how religion was really important to her and she didn't want to sin? Both ways could still point to Jack. "And what if he led a pure life to make up for a terrible mistake he made or an accident that he felt was his fault?"

"I think you're grasping at straws. But don't worry. I want to keep going, keep finding stuff out if we can. I feel like we're doing something real and good and that we're helping to bring back who she was in some way. We're giving her justice, even if her parents and the police never did."

I can't help but smile—a real one this time—and I feel much, much better, both about myself and that we are trying to help Betty, even if we never do find out her truth.

What Brian and I have in this moment feels more real to me than anything I built with Leila over the years: truth and compassion versus walking on eggshells and waiting for the storm of Leila's temper to pass.

I eat the unmolested portion of my cookie. It tastes delicious— light and sweet and airy—just like the feeling that has replaced my heavy cloud of dread.

I wait until Friday to execute the next step of my plan. That is the only day Aunt Evelyn regularly leaves the house. Instead of heading to the grocery store with her as normal, I claim that I want to work on a paper for school. This is barely a lie, I really do have a paper to write, but it is not due until the first day of school.

Personality goal: stop lying so much.

I made strides by telling Brian the truth earlier, but I am already falling into old, bad habits. At least I can sort of blame this lie on Brian since I am on the hunt for information at his request.

Still, though, this lie is kind of bad. The reason I want Aunt Evelyn out of the house is so I can snoop. Her round trip will take approximately one hour and fifteen minutes. I have never been alone in the house before. And while I feel guilty for planning to search through Aunt Evelyn's personal possessions, I want to find any other traces of Betty I can, especially if there are more photos.

Her bedroom is where I start.

I have poked my head in here before but have never really gotten much of a look. It is Spartan in appearance, with only a bed, dresser, and end table. I take a quick glance inside the wooden jewelry box on her dresser, where there is little inside that appears to be of much value.

Her pearls are around her neck, as always. The jewelry looks like Aunt Evelyn herself: old and out of style. Plus, even though I don't really know what I am searching for, there is nothing in here that helps.

After opening the first dresser drawer and eyeballing her neatly folded granny panties, I feel like an absolute sneak. It is not like she is hiding anything, after all. I move on to the closet, but it is pretty shallow and just seems to have more clothes. There are no boxes or bins which could hold memories.

I already looked through my own bedroom thoroughly, out of boredom in my first few days as a guest, so I don't waste any time there. Aunt Evelyn cleared out the dresser and most of the closet for me before I moved in, so all I found there were a few old clothes, which could be castoffs of her own or even from the house's former residents. Probably those of my great-great-grandparents and Aunt Evelyn's sister, my own great-grandmother. Maybe holding on to them makes her feel connected to the family members she has lost.

Other than that, there are only some old books in the closet and some creepy-looking dolls. One of my chores is to dust them, and I always half expect them to blink at me.

In terms of memory-storage potential, I hit the mother lode in the other guest room.

Though she has few visitors, present company excluded, Aunt Evelyn only uses her own bedroom out of the upstairs rooms. Everything else she needs is downstairs, so she can afford to keep this room set up for family members who will probably never materialize as guests. And if she ever had a sewing room, like many women from her era, she must have torn it down years ago. I can't imagine she has much dexterity left in her hands at her age anyway.

Simple enough in appearance, with a sagging double bed covered in what appears to be a handmade quilt, she has filled the closet with boxes and Rubbermaid bins. Aunt Evelyn is no hoarder by any means, but she has lived in this house her whole life. Of course, she has tons of things. Even though the closet is neat, not everything is labeled. I imagine I will be here in a few years, helping my mom and various other relatives sort through all this after Aunt Evelyn's death.

With plenty of time left, I get down to work. I find lots more clothes, bins of old quilts and blankets, old tax forms and bank books, greeting cards, and some ancient-looking holiday decorations I have never seen, even when we have visited at the appropriate time of year. Maybe that is one of many things she has let go in her advanced age.

I am feeling a little annoyed by the lack of labels because I don't have an interest in what is inside most of these containers. And just as I am feeling guilty and rather hopeless, I find the right bin.

There is no organizational system at all here. Thousands of photographs from various decades are crammed in. Not all have made the cut to the wall of memories in the living room, so this must be where the rest have gone to die or at least rest in purgatory. She probably couldn't bring herself to throw away those smiling faces of her various nieces, nephews, and everyone else who was important to her over the span of her lifetime.

But I am not interested in most of these people.

I fan out the pictures to maximize my viewing. If there is a secret filing method and she discovers my meddling, I am confident I can come up with a story to appease her—yes, another lie. There are few photographs of Aunt Evelyn herself, especially not at her age now, but a couple of layers in, I start finding some interesting older pictures.

Here she is, laughing with other teachers in a staff photo that looks like it was taken in the eighties, plus another where she is holding a cigarette in one hand and a beer in the other, smiling broadly. Whoa. Seventies, maybe?

Her sister would have been a grandmother by then, but Aunt Evelyn was still single, like she didn't give a damn about that. This partying Aunt Evelyn is hard to match up with the creature of habit she is now, and it makes me wonder how I will change as I get older.

I take a quick photo with my phone when I find one of Aunt Evelyn with her sister, who is smiling over her baby daughter, my own grandmother. That had to have been back in the forties. Great-Grandma was young when she had her daughter, only about a year after she got married. It makes me think: if Betty had stayed friends with my great-grandma and if she had lived, her own baby would have been a playmate of my grandmother's.

If only. I keep digging.

And here it is: a photo of the three girls. It is similar to the one on the wall downstairs, but there is a boy in their midst, one who is somewhat familiar. Their heads are thrown back in laughter, except for Evelyn, whose lips are pursed into a semi-smile. Whatever the joke was, Evelyn doesn't appear as amused. Has she really changed that much over the years? She was something of an old lady even when young. Or maybe she was too young to understand the joke and felt left out. It is hard to say.

I turn the photo over, just in case there are any inscription.

My three favorite girls. J.F.

J.F.

The name hits me. James Forrester? My great-grandfather was J.F. I must have seen him in a picture somewhere before—that is why he looks familiar.

Out of all the mysterious old guys with the initials J.F. who could have been out there, I missed the most obvious one—the J.F. related to me. He must have graduated before or even after Betty and my great-grandma, so he wasn't in the yearbook.

Was my great-grandfather Betty's lover? Could he possibly be the father of her baby?

And if he *was* the father, could he have been involved in her death?

My blood runs cold.

It is a lot to wrap my head around. I don't want to tell Brian on the phone or text him the information. Could my own flesh and blood be responsible for the death of his? Even the possibility fills me with shame.

I have told Brian that I found something and we should meet to talk about it. He suggests going to Nan's, home of the ever-present caffeine and sugar fixes, but that seems too public for what I have to say. After scribbling a note to Aunt Evelyn, we agree that he will pick me up and we will go to the lake.

We settle onto towels, echoing my eerie dream sequence. I tell him my news and watch while he processes it.

With a nod, he says, "It doesn't mean he murdered her, even if he was the father. And do you really think Betty would do that to her friend? Get together with her boyfriend?"

I think back to my own—far less severe by comparison, obviously—situation with Leila. "Maybe it just kind if happened. Isn't that what they say happens with affairs? That it wasn't planned and they didn't mean to hurt anyone?"

That is more or less what I overheard from my mom's friend Sue a few years ago, while she sobbed into her chardonnay on our couch for several nights following her husband's betrayal. I liked Sue and didn't mean to eavesdrop, but I couldn't help it. She was loud. Sue didn't even sound that mad. She said he was honest with her, at least. But she was very, very hurt, and it broke my heart to see her like that, this kind woman who had gotten me a gift for every single birthday.

Brian looks pensive. "What did she say in her note again? That one she wrote in code?"

I flip through the photos on my phone and find my transcription. It is easier this way than carrying my notebook everywhere. All of my "clues" are in one place. I reread it aloud: "I cannot fathom why he is pursuing me. I am not interested in him; perhaps in another life, and only if we were free. It would be a betrayal."

"Sounds like she resisted out of loyalty to her friend but then gave in anyway. He's J.F., after all, like on the tree." I point toward the *evidence*.

"Betrayal is a pretty heavy word. Here she takes the time to write all that out in code, like she's ashamed it was even happening, but then she just goes against her friend and sleeps with him anyway? That doesn't add up to me."

"Brian, I don't know why she did it either. But it would sure explain why Aunt Evelyn has those negative feelings towards her. She's loyal to her sister. Maybe after Betty died, some people guessed that the baby was Jim's since they all hung out together? I don't know." Frustrated, I take off my slides and stick my feet in the water. I want to feel something tangible, other than these amorphous sensations of confusion and, dare I think it again, ignominy. I feel like Hawthorne, with his puritanical guilt for the sins of his forefathers.

If my great-grandfather committed a murder and got away with it, am I at all responsible? It sounds silly, but then why do I feel so guilty?

The cool water laps my ankles, and I dig my toes into the squishy mud. It is kind of gross yet soothing at the same time. And then I feel something else.

"What if Aunt Evelyn knew about the baby and the betrayal before Betty died?" I whisper, holding out the tiny object I pulled from the lake's floor, a minuscule thing that may unravel the secrets, as unpleasant as they might be.

I wipe away the grime which might have shielded it for decades and show him a pearl, a globe too much like those Aunt Evelyn wears around her neck every day.

She is sitting on the couch, calm as always, with the TV blaring when I arrive back at the house. This is not a cold-blooded killer, obviously. It is a sweet old lady who knits her own sweaters, a former teacher who took care of other people's kids as if they were her own. And she was a child when Betty died, only eight years old.

I am an ungrateful idiot to think there is a connection. Even Brian, relative of the deceased, who desperately wants to uncover the truth, has told me it is crazy to suspect Aunt Evelyn was involved.

As for my great-grandfather, maybe he was guilty and maybe not, though I hate to imagine he could be. He is one of the reasons I exist on this earth. It is still somehow easier to swallow than the horrible thought of young Aunt Evelyn taking the life away from her big sister's friend, even if that friend had made a choice which could hurt people. But is it truly impossible?

I need to navigate the waters carefully.

"Aunt Evelyn?" I ask, trying to keep the tremor from my voice. But my disheveled appearance probably gives away some of my stress.

I don't really want to talk to her about this, but I can't help myself. There has to be some sort of explanation. She has always been so kind to me, so generous. There is no possible way.

I can't choke out the question I want to ask, but I open my hand, revealing the small, gritty, discolored orb. "I found this at the lake. Could it be yours? Didn't you say you had lost some pearls from your necklace once?"

Aunt Evelyn mutes the television and takes it from my palm. Her touch is cool and dry against my sweaty skin. "It doesn't look like mine, does it, dear?"

She places the new addition on the coffee table, careful to set it just right so it won't roll away. Aunt Evelyn slowly unfastens her necklace and holds her string of carefully maintained pearls in one hand, then picks up the straggler, smaller and alien.

In comparison, it doesn't look like it came from the necklace. Brian was right, and I feel like an idiot.

"Where did you find it?" she asks.

"By the lake," I answer, looking down. I can't meet those faded blue eyes. What if she guesses what I really wanted to ask?

"It doesn't sound very ladylike to go digging around at the lake, Callie," she responds. Her stern, schoolteacher tone returns once again. She takes in the dirt under my fingernails, the rat's nest that is my sloppy bun. "Perhaps you need some new hobbies?"

She turns the sound back on, and I know we are done. Aunt Evelyn stares pointedly at the pearl I found until I remove the offending object—a symbol of my disloyalty.

I put it in my pocket and retreat to my room.

But it nags at me. It is not just the pearl. It could have been anyone's, or even if it was Aunt Evelyn's, Abbott Lake wasn't only the site of Betty's murder. It may have been home to dozens of picnics Evelyn innocently attended with her family, for all I know. After all, it is only two miles from her house, an easy distance for an athlete to cover. But if that were true, wouldn't she have mentioned it?

What gets to me are Betty's own words: *it would be a betrayal.* When people feel betrayed, they sometimes act way out of character. Could Aunt Evelyn's loyalty to her sister have made her mad enough to kill? But how could a child overpower a high school graduate? It doesn't seem possible.

I flip through my phone, scrolling through my various "clues" for the second time today: Betty's coded message, her formal portrait, the heart on the tree with the initials, the picture of the sisters with Betty and my great-grandfather, his message on the back.

Sure, there are hints that Betty could have had an affair with Jim, but there is nothing other than the pearl and the look on Aunt Evelyn's face in the picture to suggest that Aunt Evelyn even knew about it—if it even happened—or enacted revenge. Besides, the pearl didn't really look like hers anyway, and the face she was making in the photo could have just been an awkward moment. She never struck me as much of a laughing type.

I lie back on the bed, close my eyes, and sift through my memory to recollect some of the things Aunt Evelyn has said when the subject of "loose women" comes up. I remember her suggesting that girls had more respect for themselves back then and that they shouldn't disgrace their families. Then there was her dismissal of Betty's death as a suicide to help her family.

Even so, despite her judgmental nature, there is nothing that points to her taking it upon herself to punish Betty.

And again, she was just a kid.

But my mind won't let it go. It is early, not even dusk yet, but I close my eyes and allow myself to doze off. I can't face Aunt Evelyn's company right now, even if she isn't responsible for anyone's death.

I have only been asleep for a short time, I think, when it strikes me.

The crucifix. Betty wore a crucifix around her neck in the formal portrait that was in the shoebox.

I am almost certain I saw a crucifix on a chain in Aunt Evelyn's jewelry box when I was snooping. Didn't I learn in Sunday school that Catholics traditionally wear a crucifix, while Protestants wear an empty cross?

Aunt Evelyn is nothing if not traditional, and no one in my family is Catholic.

In the picture of the four of them, it is around Betty's neck as well—I can see it when I zoom in. Just as Evelyn always wears her pearls, it appears Betty always wore her crucifix. Would they have buried her in it?

I listen, ears piqued. The TV is still on, and it is not yet 8:30. I may be able to sneak into her room and look at what is inside Aunt Evelyn's jewelry box...

It can't be.

Less than five minutes later, I am holding Betty's crucifix in my hand—the very one Aunt Evelyn must have taken off her corpse after she killed her.

As always, she is sitting on the couch, Luna on her lap. With the new knowledge of my great-great-aunt, the loving black cat now seems more like a witch's familiar than a pet.

Aunt Evelyn doesn't smile when I approach her. If my face

doesn't reveal what I know, the necklace in my hand does. I set it out on the coffee table in front of her.

"You should have left it alone." Aunt Evelyn's voice is barely a whisper. She is looking down, but then her eyes find mine with a laser focus despite their watery appearance. "I care for you, Callie. You are my blood. I am your blood, and she is not. She's dead and gone, and no one even cared until now. It was for the best. It was for family."

I am pushing my luck, but I also don't feel afraid of her. What can she possibly do to hurt me? With youth and strength on my side, I surge forward.

"How is it better that she died? You stole her life. And people *did* care. What about her parents? What about her cousin, Brian's grandfather?"

"She wanted to destroy my sister's life. Don't you see?" Aunt Evelyn strokes Luna absently, no sign of remorse on her face. "She tricked her fiancé and tried to steal what wasn't hers. Betty betrayed Lillian. If Lillian found out, it would ruin her. My sister was never strong like me. She wouldn't have been able to do what needed to be done."

Again, my mind sticks on that word, Betty's word: *betrayal.* It still seems so hard to believe. But I don't get into all that.

"I've had friends betray me too. But I never wanted them to die. And what about the baby? An innocent life, Aunt Evelyn." I can't even believe I am talking about this situation to a woman I have known my whole life, a woman from whom I have received so much kindness.

"That baby would have been a disgrace. It's better it never lived. I tried to tell her, but she wouldn't listen. If she'd agreed to get rid of the baby, it wouldn't have had to happen."

"How did you even know Betty was pregnant? Did she tell you? You were just a kid. And did she tell you Jim was the father?" Even with almost everything out on the table, literally as well as figuratively, I neglect to mention how I discovered the picture of all of them together while foraging through Aunt Evelyn's personal possessions.

"No, she didn't tell me. But we were close until I found out. She always said I was like the little sister she never had. I've always been good at reading people, and I knew she had a secret. When I confronted her, I had no idea what to expect, but she finally admitted about the pregnancy. She had the audacity to be happy about it." An ugly grimace clouds her wrinkled face. "But when I asked her who the father was, she refused to tell me. That's how I knew it was Jim.

"You think you're very clever, Callie, and I admire your intelligence. But you are also very naïve if you think Betty's death was my fault. She brought it on herself." She smiles at me, sadly, I think. "Jim never admitted that he transgressed, but I knew. He thought of me like a sister. After all, Lillian and Jim had been going steady since the seventh grade. He already felt like family to me and would be soon enough. It was always Jim and us girls, hanging around together. I knew he was sweet on Betty. I could tell by the way he looked at her, and I disapproved. But I trusted Betty would never want to hurt Lillian. I never imagined Betty would betray us like that. She wasn't fit for the cross around her neck. That's why I took it, and I've kept it as a reminder never to blame myself for what I had to do."

I decide not to get into the cross versus crucifix issue which tipped me off in the first place, but I will bring up that murder is far worse than sex before marriage.

"Jim betrayed Lillian too, if he slept with someone else. I'm not saying it was right, but you can't make Betty take all the blame. Stealing her friend's fiancé doesn't justify her death."

"Jim was a man. He trusted Betty as a friend, and he must have succumbed to a weak moment. Betty could be quite charming when she wished. Jim was a good man who made a mistake, and that good man would have wanted to do what was right. He would have married Betty and broken Lillian's heart. The baby would have ruined my sister's life. I just helped her take back what was hers." Her eyes seem to flash with vehemence.

No matter what I say, she refuses to admit being wrong. Does that make her a sociopath, to not feel guilt, or has she just been in denial all these years? I have no idea, but I won't let it go.

"You don't even know if Jim was the father! Did you ask her? Did you make sure she actually did what you thought before you killed her?" My voice may sound calm. I am not screaming, but I am trembling with the injustice of it all.

Aunt Evelyn nods her head in agreement. "She denied it. But I saw her poem, the one in the yearbook. It was proof! Brazen as anything, right there in the open, a mockery of my sister. All of that 'blue jay' nonsense and 'duty' over love, trying to say that he only stayed with my sister because he had said he would. I'll remember those words until the day I die. Betty always acted the part of the saint, writing that she'd endure the pain of losing him, but she still tried to steal him away anyway! Lillian was so good, so trusting. I can only hope her heart was spared, that she never found out."

I don't interrupt her to acknowledge how bizarre it is to analyze poetry at a time like this, but it is extremely odd. Scary too. She is still mad about a poem written so long ago, which could probably be interpreted any number of ways.

"I told her to meet me at the lake, that I wanted to talk. She knew I was angry but came anyway, even though it was midnight. I told her no one would know about us meeting and that she could tell me anything. But I already knew what she was hiding.

"She started crying when she saw it, my pistol. I always knew where my father kept it. That hussy said she didn't know why I was angry with her. As if she could get away with destroying my sister's life. I told her she had a choice, that she could choose her life or the baby's. I was willing to let her go if she agreed to get rid of the baby."

Aunt Evelyn pauses to catch her breath. Her words spill out too fast now that the truth has finally been revealed.

"All she said was that I didn't understand. She was right. I *didn't* understand how she could lower herself to do what she did. I would never understand how she could become a piece of filth and forget everything we meant to her." There is a slight tremor in Aunt Evelyn's hand when it reaches up, very uncharacteristically, to wipe the sweat from her brow. The timbre of her voice is pitched higher than usual, suggesting heightened emotions.

So maybe she feels some guilt from this, recounting her terrible story after all these years. Or is it justification? She keeps going, unable to stop the torrent of words gushing from her mouth.

"I made her walk into the water. She did just as I asked, dumbly, cooperatively. I think she thought I just wanted to scare her up until the end. At some point, she grabbed at me and broke my necklace." Aunt Evelyn smiles wryly. "I told you it broke once. I was furious. But then she stopped fighting me. I was the one with the gun, after all. Not that I needed to use it. I took her out in the lake and held her down until the bubbles stopped. And then I went back home before anyone awoke.

"They never even knew I was gone. And who would suspect a sweet little girl of being involved with such an ugly thing?" She pauses, batting her sparse eyelashes and feigning innocence. "I cried along with Lillian and Jim when Betty was found. Jim looked devastated for a few weeks, but he moved on. And he married Lillian, just as he was supposed to. He had his babies with his wife rather than his whore. And that's why you got to live on this earth, Callie. If she didn't die, you would never have lived. It was for the greater good."

I am at a loss for words. She recites this story as if she is retelling the plot of one of her TV shows, disconnected and callous.

"There must have been a hundred other ways to make sure Betty didn't ruin your sister's life," I finally say. "Why not just tell her to go away? She was about to leave for nursing school anyway. Why did she have to die?"

"I was strong, and she was weak. She was a bad, weak girl who needed to go away." She zeroes in on me with eyes that no longer have any shred of warmth in them. "You are a bad, weak girl who needs to go away."

Time slows, like the air has become gelatinous and thick. The woman who has said this has previously told me she loves me and is proud of me. She has consoled me and wiped away my tears when I was little and scraped my knee. Aunt Evelyn has sent me birthday and Christmas cards every year of my life. But now?

Now she fingers the barrel of a small pistol she has seemingly conjured from thin air.

I hate, hate, hate, hate guns. Everyone at my school remembers the day during freshman year when Larry Briscoe didn't make it to class. He had accidentally—we assume—shot himself while fooling around with his dad's gun. Larry never got to come back to school again, his life cut short at fourteen.

And now my great-great-aunt is pointing a gun at me.

I open my mouth to speak, but I have no voice, can only choke out a faint sound that isn't even a word. But I stand up, not knowing what will happen, hoping this is all a bad dream, that I will wake feeling ashamed to have had such negative thoughts about my elderly relative.

My heartbeat drums in my ears. How much longer will that

heart get to beat?

Although I am never impulsive, although I haven't thought about the consequences, I flee from the room and out of the house.

I make my getaway, running past the weeping willow tree which once offered me comfort. Now I just feel an aching, black void in my heart. Everything is different now.

Every single thing.

The door bangs shut, and I am grateful for the cover of night, with only the faint luster of the full moon. Aunt Evelyn knows I can't have gotten far, but she obviously won't be able to catch me on foot. I curse myself for leaving my iPhone. There is no one I can turn to for help, and I can't run very fast in these slides.

Tears and snot trickle down my face. I kick off my stupid, cumbersome shoes, get off the street, and run though the field. Though I am hardly able to see, I can feel every single rock and root under my feet, shredding my skin like tissue paper. I fall and my skin burns, but I get up and keep running.

Aunt Evelyn will find me, and I know that. She called me weak, but she is wrong. I will not stop fighting for my life.

There are the headlights of the car I so recently thought of as my own. I stop running when I see where we are: Abbott Lake, of course.

CHAPTER

FIFTEEN

The lake shimmers in the moonlight, serene as always, the dark water ready to cover up secrets and pearls and girls.

In the glare of the headlights, I stay frozen and wait for Evelyn to get out of the car. I can no longer think of her as *Aunt Evelyn*. Even if biology dictates that is who she is, I won't claim her now that I know for sure what she has done, what she wants to do to me.

I am so tired. My body hurts, along with my mind and heart. It feels heavy, like a sponge filled to capacity, and I want to be wrung out, squeezed dry of my thoughts and emotions. I would prefer emptiness in my heart to the way it feels now, full of lead.

Not literally. Not yet, at least.

She stops the car and gets to her feet, an atypical criminal, stooped and frail. But her malice, her intent, are written in the deep, shadowed grooves of her face.

I find my voice. "Please don't do this. Think what you'll do to my mom. Even if I've offended or wronged you, she never has, but this will kill her." I hate the whine in my voice, but I don't want to die. I want to live, to start my senior year in a few weeks, even if I am friendless. Their words can't hurt me like her bullet can.

"It will hurt her, you're right. But I will not let you come to my home as my guest and ruin my life. I have a reputation, and you will not destroy it," she says, like I am the one who has created this mess. "Bad, weak girls must go away."

The moonlight catches the metal of the pistol in her hand.

The whole thing is just plain dumb. She is seriously going to murder me to protect her reputation? The person who almost never leaves her house and is eighty-nine years old?

"What will you say? How will you possibly get away with a dead seventeen-year-old on your hands?" I start off emboldened but then try to appeal to her logical side. "I won't tell. Just call my mom and tell her you don't want me here anymore. Say whatever you want. You'll never have to see me again, I promise. I'll go away on my own. Really."

Evelyn shifts her weight, but the pistol in her hand remains steady. "But it's never that simple with you, is it, Callie? Here, I take you in as a guest to get away from your troubled life. I try to help, but you're too damaged. No one will never think I had anything to do with it. They didn't think a little girl could kill, and they won't think an old lady will either.

"It's a simple story. You broke into my gun box and stole it while I slept. Scared at the thought of your impending return to school, where you aren't wanted, you decided to end things in much the same manner as the woman with whom you became obsessed. I found your clipping. I'm sure the police will be interested in it when they try to figure out why you did it."

She starts walking closer to me while she says it. How is this possibly happening to me? I actually might die, at Abbott Lake of all places, and I am crying and pleading with her not to do it, to please just let me go away on my own, when I see it.

In the lake. I see *it* in the lake.

An object.

No, not a thing. It is a person.

And they begin to move.

It moves even though it shouldn't be moving, can't be moving, because it can't exist. She hasn't existed for more than eighty years.

Betty lifts her head from the water and looks at Evelyn. And she starts coming closer to us.

Betty is not gliding or floating, or anything graceful, like I expected a ghost would. I don't know what she is, but I know it is her. What I can see of her skin is pale in the moonlight, but at least she has skin. This can't be her actual body reanimated. Her own flesh would be long since gone, rotted away. I shiver despite the warmth of the humid night.

This is really happening.

Her gait is lumbering, as if the weight of the water is heavy on her limbs. Or maybe she is out of practice in terms of moving, having not done so for so long. I still don't know what I am seeing, but I know that it is her.

She is hardly the smiling girl from the photographs, but I recognize her, even with her sodden hair and disjointed movements. And, as crazy as it sounds, when she turns her gaze to me, it seems like she recognizes me.

When those dark, dead eyes lock into mine, there is kindness and understanding in them. I can see that even from yards away. It is as if she knows how I have struggled to find out what happened to her, to hear her voice across the decades. It is like she knows I have had pain and hurt and betrayal as well.

We are two teenagers from different eras, one alive and one dead. But there is enough tying us together to make the charge between us almost electric.

I am no longer scared, not frightened of Betty, not even of Evelyn. It dawns on me that maybe Betty is here to help me.

When I finally look back at Evelyn, her face has twisted in horror. She is slack-jawed and has dropped her pistol, assumed a nearly hunch-backed pose. Betty lurches closer and closer. I am not the damsel in distress, but a spectator while the villain prepares to receive her comeuppance.

Betty reaches the shore and stands or hovers directly in front of Evelyn. She seems transformed. No longer a dead or ghostlike thing, she radiates light and beauty. I can't tell if her luminescence is internal or a trick of the light.

She glistens while she opens her mouth and says, "You will not steal another life."

Has Betty always been here, waiting for me, or waiting for Evelyn? Either way, she is my savior, and she is glorious. Betty picks up the pistol and throws it into the lake. It is no longer a living thing, a threat.

Every second stretches on. I have no idea what will happen, but I am safe. Evelyn practically croaks out her words when she looks into her victim's eyes.

"You would have stolen Lillian's life. I couldn't allow it." But the passion, the anger, are gone, and her words sound small and weightless in the night.

Although she has had decades to contemplate it—if she has been able to think during all this time rather than spending the ensuing years on some other plane of existence, or maybe nowhere at all—Betty doesn't seem angry, exactly. I don't know what I expect her to do to her killer, but it is not out of any scary movie I have ever seen.

All Betty says is, "I never did that. Lillian was my best friend. No matter what you thought, no matter what you still think, I never betrayed you or your sister. I tried to tell you. I was going to tell you everything. But you never gave me the chance."

She lowers her voice and whispers something, but I can't hear over the ribbiting frogs and rustling leaves around me.

Evelyn seems to soften for a moment and reaches out her hand. Betty continues to talk quietly, but something starts to happen.

Evelyn opens her mouth, but her jaw sort of becomes unhinged. She looks like she is going to step forward, but she collapses onto the ground.

Betty drops to Evelyn's side. "Take her to the hospital," she says.

And it is truly the strangest night of my life—a teenage ghost commands me to help her killer, who happens to be my elderly relative who was threatening to kill me.

Betty didn't wield any magical ghost powers to make this

happen or steal Evelyn's life force. Maybe it was Evelyn's own guilty conscience finally being activated after all these years. Perhaps her body contained her secret too long and couldn't hold up anymore. Whatever just occurred, I can't fathom how Evelyn's victim would have any desire to let her live. But I decide to do what Betty tells me anyway.

Betty helps me move Evelyn's limp, tiny body into the passenger seat of the car. Why doesn't Betty just want me to call 911? But they probably didn't have that back then, let alone cellphones, and I have no idea if she understands how the world has changed since she left it. I don't have my phone on me anyway.

My adrenaline is high, and my brain swarms with mixed emotions. I am simply confused.

Just as I think Betty is about to get into the car with me, she shakes her head. "I can only show myself here."

There are a thousand questions I want to ask her, this remarkable woman/girl/ghost who is sad for the loss of her life but wants her murderer to live for some reason. But she is hurrying me along.

"Will I see you again?" I ask, like a romantic fool after my first date with the mysterious man of my dreams.

She smiles sadly. "I'm afraid not. But I wanted to thank you for everything. Thank you for seeing me."

I am not positive, but I think she means for caring, for understanding her story, rather than physically seeing the apparition before me, which raises a thousand more questions. Who put that clipping in the book in the first place? Was she watching us all this time? Who was the baby's father, if she maintains it wasn't my great-grandfather? And why would she want to save Evelyn?

But all she says is, "Uncover."

I think that is what she says, but it is garbled, and I am getting a blinding stress-induced headache. Somehow, I am driving my would-be killer to the hospital. Betty's figure lingers in the rearview mirror, but the light is quickly expunged, a candle snuffed out, and I know she is gone.

I drive on in the darkness.

Illustration by Amanda Bergloff

CHAPTER

SIXTEEN

There are so many questions, of course, at the hospital because I didn't call to let them know I was coming. I tell the staff that Evelyn and I were walking around the property when she keeled over. Then I rushed to get the car but couldn't remember where my phone was to call 911 since I was so worried.

Some of the nurses look at me like I am the dumbest teenager on earth, but they attend to her and take her away. A hospital employee tosses me that weird anemone-looking keychain an hour or so later while I am in the waiting room. I assume he parked the car.

They make me call my parents, which I really don't want to do, but I am not interested in talking to a social worker, so it is what it is. Luckily, I can't deal with trying to explain things yet, and my mom agrees not to come that night since it is already so late. She is sort of freaking out, but I assure her that I am okay.

"Mom, we knew she's super old. It's not that surprising that this happened," I say, leaving out everything we didn't know about

Evelyn and what we never in a million years would have guessed.

I sit numbly in the waiting room, not knowing what I am waiting for, not knowing what I want Evelyn's outcome to be.

She was going to kill me, probably. I don't know if she really would have, but she pointed a gun at me, brandished a pistol, like in one of her Westerns. Evelyn admitted to drowning her sister's best friend for something the girl claimed she didn't do, and I believe Betty now, even if I wasn't so sure before.

When the doctor finally tells me that Evelyn has had a stroke, that she is resting right now but can't see me, I am incredibly relieved. She will be here at the hospital for the next few days for monitoring. The doctor says I can visit tomorrow but that I should go home.

Do I want her to die? Do I want her to pay for what she did to Betty and Betty's child? What she had wanted to do to me?

I don't know. I just want to sleep.

So, I drive "home," to the place where I have been welcomed by my would-be murderer. Without even showering off the grime and sweat, I climb into the four-poster bed and fall into a dreamless sleep, the best gift my mind and body could possibly give me on such an occasion.

CHAPTER

SEVENTEEN

Forgive.

I step out of the shower after an attempt to wash away more than the physical reminders of my night before. This one word is written on the mirror. Though it is gone when I rub my eyes and look again, I think it was Betty reaching out one last time. She said she could only show herself at the lake, but maybe she has some other abilities. Perhaps I just imagined it, but maybe not.

Such a simple word but full of meaning. It gives me some things to think about.

And not just regarding Evelyn.

Mom is arriving around 2:00 p.m. to see me and visit the hospital, so obviously, I need to sort through some things before she gets here. Brian should know what happened...*everything* that happened. I am dying to talk about it all with someone who cares.

After texting him that I need to tell him some stuff, I take the car and drive to his house. Sure, he could come here. Then I wouldn't have to worry about the possibility of his grandfather being around to hear everything. I don't know what all we should tell Mr. Spencer about this, if anything, but I really don't want to be in Evelyn's house a minute longer than necessary. Since she was the danger, it feels haunted by her, even without her presence.

When Brian and I last spoke, it was with the understanding that I was going to try to figure out whether or not the pearl belonged to Evelyn. Brian had acted shocked that I would even go there in my imagination, let alone verbalize it or confront Evelyn.

Clearly, there is a lot to catch him up on.

While he can't possibly know what I have been through, when he opens the door and sees me standing there, I guess some of the ordeal is written on my face. Despite how much time we have spent together, we have rarely had any physical contact, but he pulls me in for a hug, and I let him hold me for a minute before I pull away.

I need this, after everything: a reminder that I am important to someone. After your own flesh and blood tries to kill you, it is pretty crucial to have this. A couple of tears might have squeezed out of my eyes, but I get myself together because I want to talk more than I need to cry.

We sit together at the wooden kitchen table. Brian plays host and fixes us both some coffee. He even puts out cookies. They are not homemade, but I am touched that he places them on a little ceramic tray. I mean, there is a snowman on it, and it is a just simple gesture during the drama of everything that has unfolded, but I appreciate it all the same.

Brian's grandpa deserves to hear this story too, but I need to talk to my friend first. When Willy nuzzles his great yellow snout into my hands, though, I don't object to his company at all and run my fingers through his thick fur. He settles next to me, sliding to the floor with an audible sigh. Dogs just know stuff sometimes, and he is there to comfort me.

An hour later, after I have told Brian everything and he has asked a ton of questions, he is still really and truly shocked.

"I wish I had seen her too," he says after a long pause. "I would've really liked to meet her."

I stare at him. He is acting almost jealous, like I ran into a celebrity and he missed out. He is missing the part where I almost got killed. But then again, Betty was his blood relative, just like the person who made her into a ghost is mine.

"Okay, I can see how you'd say that—she was really something, after all—but did you not hear the part about Evelyn being a murderer and also trying to add to the body count? What do I even do about that? Do I tell my mom everything? Do we call the cops? If Evelyn makes it out of the hospital, does she go to jail?"

He is quiet again. "I think it's time for the truth, Callie. I think it's time to let everything out."

And he is right. Maybe I don't want my mom to be upset, but she and I can't go on in a world of fiction. It is time to tell her the truth about everything.

So, when she arrives at Evelyn's house later that afternoon, that is exactly what I do.

I tell her what happened. *All* of it.

CHAPTER

EIGHTEEN

We sit in the living room, and I think back to Evelyn's comment on the first day I stayed there: if these walls could talk. And while we are anthropomorphizing the walls, what would they think about what I am going to tell my mom? Is it disloyal to Evelyn to reveal her secrets while I am sitting on her throne?

Forget it—I am done with secrets and the lies we tell to protect them.

Mom remains tight-lipped through most of it. I start with what I have learned of Betty and Evelyn, taking her through my pictures and showing her Betty's sketchbook, as well as the newspaper clipping. She needs to see and understand how I figured it out, that I am not just jumping to a crazy conclusion based on an overactive imagination or some sick revenge scheme to hurt her for sending me here.

When I describe the whole ghost thing, I am positive she will have a psychiatrist on speed dial for me, ready to send the men in white coats to take me away, but she sits very still and listens.

After I finish, she begins sobbing. Mom is not a really emotional person. She doesn't cry during movies practically ever, so this kind of takes me by surprise. I don't know what she is crying for.

"Do you believe me? Or do you think I'm crazy?" I ask after I have given her a glass of water, some tissues, and a few minutes to compose herself.

I am still so mixed up from all of it that I don't even know how to feel, and I have had more time than she has to process it. It is all true because I was actually there, but I can't imagine what I would think if someone just told me about it.

"I don't want to believe you." Her voice sounds raw, as if she has been screaming, bearing the weight of everything she has just absorbed. "She's my aunt. Well, my great-aunt. But you're my daughter. Callie?" Her eyes, already red under hooded, puffy lids, search for mine.

"Yeah?"

Is this the part where she tells me it is time for therapy? After everything, I might be inclined to agree. It has been a tough few months, with last night acting as the icing on the extremely crappy cake.

"Callie, I believe you. I recognize her. Betty." She fingers the crucifix in front of her. "I saw her when I was your age, when I stayed here with Evelyn. I saw her in my dreams when I slept in that stupid four poster bed. I dreamt of her at the lake. I just didn't know who she was or why I kept dreaming about her. I think she's been waiting for someone to learn her story for a long time. I wonder if I let her down since I didn't ever do anything."

Now it is my time to console her. "What could you do? As far as you knew, she was a figment of your imagination."

"I haven't thought of it in years. But it's as if I could've dreamed about her last night." She pauses. "We need to tell the police. We'll just leave out the ghost stuff, okay?"

Mom ends up staying several days, having called off work due to a family emergency, which is exactly what it is. In different ways.

She has been to the hospital but doesn't ask me to go, and I don't offer. What could I say to the woman who wanted me dead? *Hey, hope you get better so you can try to kill me again?* I don't wish death upon Evelyn. After all, her own victim wants me to forgive her. But I don't want to see her either. The wound is too fresh.

Mom updates me on her status, though. The doctors said Evelyn's brain went for a long time without oxygen, so her recovery time may be prolonged. She will probably never again be fully functional.

I don't grill Mom about what she said to her. Who knows if Evelyn could even hear or understand her, based on the poor condition she is currently in. Maybe I will ask Mom someday, but processing the change from kindly relative to would-be daughter murderer, actual murderer of a ghost who has visited your dreams, can't be an easy thing, even for a strong and intelligent woman like my mom.

We go to the cops, all of us—my mom, Brian, his granddad, and me—show them our evidence, and tell them everything, except Betty's foray back into the present. I am trying not to lie anymore, but I truly think this omission is a good thing. Otherwise, they won't take anything seriously.

I tell them how I confronted Evelyn about the murder and ran to Abbott Lake, where she tracked me down. Then I threw the pistol in the lake when Evelyn collapsed, but that part is a lie, of course.

Since they don't have any reason, that I am aware of, to believe I lied, will they even check? They won't find my own fingerprints. Would they find Betty's? I don't know if ghosts have fingerprints, and maybe they will all be washed away. I will never know, and I guess it doesn't really matter that much.

They believe the story and will formally press charges once Evelyn is out of the hospital. *If* she comes out of the hospital. So, the legal side of the story is wrapped up, for now anyway, unless I need to give testimony at some point.

Nevertheless, it's time for me to move on.

One way I am supposed to try to accomplish this is by meeting up with a therapist once I get back home. I am not super excited to discuss my mixed-up feelings to anyone, let alone a stranger, but Mom has convinced me it can't hurt. It might help, which sounds fair enough to me. Some people swear by it, and I have definitely had the most challenging time in my life over the last few months. So, I agree to a minimum of five sessions to see what I think.

It was rough for Mom to talk to me about that. She is always so worried about not making anything harder for me. That is why she didn't press me when I was going through all the bad stuff at school. She wanted me to feel safe at home, but we probably should have talked about it when it all went down.

I ended up telling her everything that happened with Leila and other friends from school, but she already knew most of it.

Go figure.

Mom and I pretty much agree that we need to do a better job of communicating with each other in general. We want to stop keeping so many secrets in the family.

With everything out in the open and senior year almost ready to start, Mom asks if I want to transfer to a new school. I give it some thought, but it is not what I want.

Forget that. I will walk in, head held high, on my first day of my senior year, and I will do well in my classes. Maybe I will join some different clubs to find some new friends. And if I don't fit in, it is just one more year.

But I am not going to drown in my sorrows anymore. I won't let the cruelty of high school do me like that.

Speaking of Leila, she actually reached out to me. The timing was awful, of course, with everything else going on, but leave it to Leila to think everything revolves around her. I can't say I am that surprised when the text arrives.

A simple *Hey*, as if nothing ever happened.

Let me just state that I hate that as a text. Hey? Come on. It is just stupid all by itself. Of course, I don't respond.

A few minutes later, Leila follows up with: *Its me. Derek told me he kissed u, so we broke up and im not mad at u anymore.*

Just like that. Not even an apology. And she thinks everything can go back to being the same? As if she hadn't broken me? As if she has had the right to be angry all this time?

But I remember Betty's advice on the mirror: *Forgive.*

And after all the grown-up talks I have had with Mom, I sort of feel like I never should have given Leila that power over me in the first place. She only broke me because I let her. I can't go back to that, but it is pointless to argue, useless to show her how she was wrong. Why give her anything more to use as ammunition against me?

After receiving a few more texts which contain zero apologies, I finally respond: *Still out of town, but I'll see you when school starts.*

It is not accusatory, but it also doesn't invite further communication.

I am hoping we will leave it at that.

The night after I hung out with the police all day, I sit up straight in bed after a fitful sleep. Yep, it is 12:17. It strikes me now that this is probably the time when Betty died all those years ago. Evelyn said they met at the lake at midnight. I guess it took her all of seventeen minutes to extinguish Betty's life forever.

If I dreamt about Betty, I don't remember it. But there is one thought on my mind when I wake up, a thought that has been mulling around in my brain for the last forty-eight hours or so. It has finally broken free: *uncover.* That was Betty's last spoken word to me.

There is still something she wants me to figure out, and the clue must be in her shoebox. This can't wait until morning. I have to call Brian.

Now.

With all that has gone on, I don't feel too guilty for sneaking out of the house while Mom snores away in the other guest room. She chose the smaller, lumpier bed rather than sleep in the room of the woman who wanted to murder her firstborn.

Sure, I could wake her up and let her be a part of this, but I really think Brian and I have to be the ones to find whatever Betty wanted us to discover. Betty would want it that way.

It strikes me as funny. Brian and I are Betty's peers now, though she would be almost a hundred if alive. Poor Betty will forever be a teenager.

I walk to the end of the cul-de-sac so Mom won't hear Brian's truck. The shoebox I told him to bring is on the floor in the back seat.

I climb in and say, "I think we need to go there. To the lake."

He nods. "She lived and died there. And it's where you saw her and where she saved you. Whatever the deal is, I think you're right. And maybe she'll show herself again?"

The eagerness swells in his voice, but I believe Betty is done with Abbott Lake, even though Betty did say it was a place she could show herself. Why come back now that her killer is finally going to be put to justice?

We are there in just a couple of minutes. Brian and I ride in silence with a singular goal: to find the final clue. He shuts off the engine but turns on the overhead light. Without saying a word, he hands me the shoebox.

Although we have been through it before and, therefore, know what to expect, we are obviously missing something. I take out the familiar objects, one by one. Most are straightforward. There is not much to glean from a pair of gloves or movie tickets. Not even the baby blanket gives anything away, even though I am sure Betty made it with love.

There is only one item which really gives us a window into Betty's inner world, and that is her sketchbook.

I have looked at the photos of her drawings, the code, and her book reviews countless times, but there is something special about holding the volume in my hands. My fingers slide over the thick, three-dimensional cover carefully constructed by Betty all those years ago.

Poor Betty. When she was attaching the lace and fastening these pieces of jewelry way back when, she never would have imagined her fate. It is a marvel it remained so pristine, that the glue—or however else it is held together—did its job long after her death.

Uncover.

I open the sketchbook and examine the inside cover, where the fabric meets the leather. And I pull.

"Callie! What are you doing? Don't wreck it." Brian reaches for the journal to take it back from me.

Under the cover.

The fabric lifts easily, the glue loosening its hold. I hold my breath. Either I am about to find a hidden clue, or I am ruining Betty's special sketchbook.

"I think there's something inside." I close the book and continue to remove the wrapping.

An unsealed envelope is buried underneath.

My fingers shake while I reach inside it, finding a piece of paper and a ring.

A wedding ring?

I hold it out to Brian, and we inspect it together. A simple gold band. It has to be a wedding ring.

Huh?

"She was married? But why hide it?" I ask.

"And why not tell? Then Evelyn wouldn't have thought she had a thing with your great-grandpa."

"Let's not speculate before we check out the note." I open the paper, stiff with age, and read the unfamiliar script aloud:

Fort Dix, New Jersey
My querida,
July 1, 1943

How I miss you, though it has been but weeks since I saw you last. Do not worry so much about me. The days are long and hard, but I am learning how to be a soldier for our country. Most of the other men are treating me okay, though some have been cruel. I am the only Mexican American in my unit.

I still do not know where they will send me after basic training is done, but our separation is temporary while our union is forever. I will think of you and our growing baby inside you. I know you will both await me when I finally come home.

I wish we could have shared our joy with your

family before I left. My heart aches to think that your parents do not know or approve of our love. Your grandfather is a fine man, and I hope that he can accept that we are together and that he will help mend relations with your parents. We are man and wife in the eyes of the Lord as well as the law, and that is enough for me for now.

I look at your photograph every night before I close my eyes for sleep and pray that you and our baby are safe. Your letters mean everything to me. Te amo.

Your husband,
Juan

Brian and I just stare at each other. The paper curls in my hand.

"They were married," I say after processing what I have read. "If Betty told the truth, Evelyn wouldn't have killed her. She had this whole love story, but Evelyn turned it into something tainted. And not even true."

"I guess her parents didn't approve, so she kept it hidden. But why from her friends? Maybe because he was Mexican? And how did he know Betty's grandfather?" Brian lets out an exasperated sigh. "It's so infuriating, all of it. We know now about the baby's father, but it just makes the story sadder. I wonder if anyone contacted him or if he ever even made it home after the war."

"I guess this is the final piece we get to the puzzle, and we need to leave it here. That's all she said: *uncover*. Or maybe 'under the cover.' Maybe she wanted us to know that she wasn't messing around with anyone else's guy. But yeah, there are a lot of unanswered questions, still." I hold up the ring to the light. "I wonder if she ever wore this. She sure kept a lot of secrets, and I know that her parents didn't approve, but I hope she let herself have some happiness."

And then something catches my eye. An almost familiar inscription inside the band: *B.B. + J.E.*

J.F. wasn't even J.F. It was J.E.

On my phone, I scroll to the picture I took of the initials on the tree: *B.B. + J.F.* I zoom in. Could it be J.E.? It had to be. I guess Juan or Betty, whoever carved it, didn't put as much force on the bottom bar of the E.

"So, it was the tree guy after all, even if we got the initials wrong. Juan E. How many Juan E.'s could there possibly be in Deerville, Pennsylvania, in 1943? And if her grandparents knew him, that means maybe my grandpa knew him? But he was just a kid, so probably not. And he never said anything before about some guy who could be the father. And she was obviously keeping the secret of her relationship from several people, at the very least."

The annoyance is plain on Brian's face while his stream of consciousness spills out.

"Why did she leave us all these clues about her life but not enough to fit the pieces together? I'm sick of this, and I don't get what she wants us to know. And meanwhile, she can just pop back into existence as a ghost or whatever." He throws his hands in the air, frustrated.

But I don't quite see it the same way. I take a minute before I say anything, attempting to figure it out.

"I think this might be the part where that expression 'Let sleeping dogs lie' comes into play, Brian. Maybe she's told us everything she wanted to. We know Evelyn killed her, we know she didn't betray Lillian, and we know she was secretly married to the father of her baby. She didn't do anything to hurt anyone, and she saved my life by throwing the gun away after Evelyn saw her. Whether Juan lived or died, well, maybe that's not a part of her story since she and the baby weren't there if or when he came back. There was no happily ever after for them."

We agree to leave it at that—for the night, at least.

It is sort of an embarrassing talk with Mrs. King at Briar Creek Manor bright and early the next morning, explaining how I need to quit without giving my two weeks' notice since Evelyn is still in the hospital and my parents can't have me living in Deerville by myself as a minor. However, she is nice enough about it, especially since I am going to work my shift that day and next week's schedule hasn't been set.

I feel bad about it. It will mean extra craziness for my coworkers, but I have been through a lot, after all. And there is only so much time Mom can take off from work at such short notice.

While Evelyn's evil deed will undoubtedly be unveiled in the local newspaper in the coming weeks, I stick with the simple story to my boss, and I am not telling any lies. Evelyn had a stroke. That is totally legit, and Mrs. King probably doesn't want to know that whole part about my life being threatened anyway. I will let her worry about all the other elderly people of Deerville, and the doctors and police can deal with Evelyn.

Mrs. King doesn't share my news before my shift begins an hour later.

I go through the motions one last time, making sure to be extra friendly to the residents while I pour their tea and coffee. It is kind of sad knowing it is the last time I will hear Mr. Danvers asking for his Sweet'N Low, so I try to commit his voice, which is coincidentally both sweet and low, to my memory. I have no such caring thoughts for Mrs. Kraemer, the mean lady who thought I was Betty that one day, even though she has been completely benign ever since.

At the end of my shift, when I finish loading and getting scalded by the evil dishwasher for the very last time, I experience no sense of loss to leave this job. I am not sure what I want to do as a career later in life, but I know for certain it is not this.

When I go to leave, I take the coward's way out and don't tell anyone. No sense upsetting the delicate balance that is my coworkers' collective temperament. I simply say goodbye and walk down the hall toward the door which leads to my freedom.

And yet, there is something that holds me back.

I can't place it at first, with all the hustle and bustle of workers' and residents' voices, the scraping of walkers and wheelchairs, and the beeping of machines keeping the patients alive and functional. It is faint at first, coming from a hallway I haven't ventured into during my service.

It can't be, and yet it is.

Before I walk any further and actually see his name on the door, I know I have found him. Or she has found him for me. It is that same song playing at low volume, almost imperceptible under the layers of other noises: "Moonlight Cocktail."

The nameplate on the door reads "Juan Espinoza." All this time, he has been right here, under my nose.

CHAPTER

NINETEEN

The door is open, which is typical for this time of the day. How fortunate it is that he happens to be playing this song at exactly this moment, just as I am about to walk out of this building forever. Then again, has any of this really been about coincidence?

He is ancient and shriveled-looking in an oversize sweater, sitting in a plush armchair in the rather austere bedroom, visible to me while I stand in his doorway. I rap lightly on the door, unsure of what on earth to say. This is my final task for Betty. I almost stop myself, thinking maybe I should tell Brian and we can visit together. But listening to the song makes me take this step. It is a song I have never heard in my life before this summer.

My appearance fails to register much of a reaction from Mr. Espinoza, whose name isn't one I recognize despite my familiarity with the residents and their dietary needs. He signals with his hand for me to come inside.

With Brian, Mr. Spencer, and the awful Mrs. Kraemer feeling like I resemble Betty, I certainly don't want her own widower thinking that as well. It might be too painful for him to bear. My sea-green, stained Briar Creek Manor uniform top and white pants barely distinguish me from many of the other workers. He must assume I am an orderly or something. Hopefully, I don't look much like the beauty he remembers.

That would be a good thing, in my opinion. It could all just be too much.

"Yes, young lady?" Mr. Espinoza picks the arm off the record player, abruptly stopping the music. He has just the trace of an accent.

I am just standing there dumbly and looking around his room. Despite his frail appearance, he seems dignified, with his heavy white mustache and large glasses under which two winged eyebrows try to fly away.

Well, why not just spill it? I have never been in a resident's room before, and I am not supposed to be. My time may be limited. Someone who knows better may come any moment and shoo me away.

I decide to go for it.

"Were you married to Betty Bryson?"

He sits there without changing his expression for so long I don't know if he heard me. At his advanced age, considering he is a resident of a nursing home, he may suffer from any number of cognitive impairments.

But he adjusts his glasses and says in an almost strangled voice, "However did you come to know that?"

What else can I do? I tell him.

I tell him all of it without holding anything back. Mr. Espinoza doesn't interrupt me or ask any questions, doesn't express outrage or doubt. He just listens.

Mr. Espinoza has lived so long that maybe the complexity of life—and even the afterlife—fails to shock him.

When I am done, he buries his face in his hands. His body shakes violently, and a long, low wail pervades the room. It seems to come from everywhere, not just his body, but from the walls themselves.

Part of me feels intrusive for witnessing this poor man's grief, for unraveling the mystery of so long ago, but I feel so close to Betty after everything. I am glad I am able to help in this way.

Mr. Espinoza soon composes himself and thanks me. "I've waited a long, long time to find out what happened to them." He surely means both Betty and the baby. "Now I finally know."

And then I wait for him to tell me his story, which he does.

CHAPTER

TWENTY

I came to America in 1941, when I was eighteen years old, with my brother and some other men. Our parents had died, and we thought Mexico had nothing for us anymore, so we left when the enganchadores, the labor recruiters, came to our village, promising wealth and riches in America.

How could we know what awaited us there? We saw it as our chance and left with many others from neighboring villages to work in a steel mill. But it was a terrible place, with harsh conditions and dreadful dangers, and we did not make the money to afford a lifestyle with many comforts.

When a white friend told me he was leaving to work on a farm so his lungs could breathe clean air again, I went with him. My brother stayed, saying the life was good enough for him and that he did not need more. I asked him to come, but he would not.

We had farmed in Mexico, working on a rich man's land, so the work in Deerville was easy for me. The farmer was kind, even offering the laborers dwelling space within the barn. I worked *hard but ate well. It was a satisfying enough existence, and I grew strong and broad compared to the skinny boy who had left Mexico. But I soon grew lonely.*

I never meant to outstay my welcome or overstep my station. Betty was an only child with little attention from her parents, so she often came to her grandparents' farm to spend time with them, the animals, and her young cousin.

Of course, I noticed her right away. She was beautiful and kind. I was too shy to speak with her since my English was so poor at the time. But I watched her kindness from afar, in the way she spoke with the people and cared for the farm animals. She was gentle with the cows while she milked them, always laughing and happy when she fed the chickens.

I used to count down the days until she would come again, all the while studying my English dictionary and reading the few worn copies of books I could find at the five and dime store in town.

And I knew my place. As a young, poor Mexican immigrant with little formal education, I could not presume, in those days, to win the love of the granddaughter of a wealthy landowner. But eventually, she noticed.

It was near dusk, and the other men had stopped work for the day, but I had a few more tasks to complete to ensure the horses were properly bedded down for the night. While I fetched clean water and picked their hooves, I sensed someone watching me. When I turned around, I saw her sitting in the haystack, capturing my likeness while I went about my work. She carried her journal everywhere.

Betty was embarrassed when I caught her sketching me, I could tell. But she introduced herself, like the lady she was, as if I didn't already know her name. Much later, she told me she had seen me watching her and that was one of the reasons she took an interest in me. She said I looked honest, hardworking, and handsome. It's funny how people are drawn together so often by appearance, but what makes them stay together runs so much deeper.

To this day, I wonder what our lives would have been like had we been given the chance to grow old together. But our time was short.

I asked to see her drawing, in my broken English, and she bashfully showed me. Though I had watched her sketching so many times, I was amazed by her talent and intrigued at discovering more about her.

We began stealing time together. Betty and I both knew the men on the farm would not approve, so our friendship began in secret. She came to the farm more frequently and helped me with my English. Betty had so much passion for life! She wanted to draw, become a nurse, read books, and travel to other lands. Betty yearned for knowledge and beauty and adventure. She helped me see what I could not before: that there was more to life than just getting by with food to eat and a place to sleep.

We sneaked away to be alone whenever we could. There was a lake we went to, the lake you mentioned. I carved our initials in a tree—my own way to declare our love in a world that forced us to keep it secret. But I guess I didn't do a good enough job with my carving, though, if my E looked like an F to you.

But anyway, she drew me there, once, in her sketchbook. When she wasn't reading or talking about changing the world, she was always drawing.

When I found out the baby was coming, I begged her to marry me. Our love was true, and we would both want our baby to be legitimate. She was still in high school but was eighteen, so she could marry without her parents' consent, especially back in those days, when the laws were different.

Betty wanted their blessing but feared their reaction. Of course, I already knew her grandparents, but they had no idea of our relationship, and I left it to Betty to tell her family about me when she was ready.

I borrowed a truck, and we drove to Maryland, to a small chapel where we could marry quickly. While I can't recall after all these years exactly what she told her parents about where she was, I know she did not tell the truth. Her father disliked Mexicans, though his wife's father, at least, could see me for a good man.

As far as I know, she never told them about me.

I had no one to tell except my brother, so I wrote him a letter that we would be married, and he met us there. We waited the mandatory time after applying for our license and had our small ceremony. Betty wore a simple ivory dress, I remember, and wove flowers into her hair. She cried because she could not have her mother or friends there with her, but she was too worried that they would try to stop her. Betty said that once we were married, everyone would learn to live with it, especially after the baby came.

The absence of her friends and family hung like a dark cloud over our special day, but we were happy. We exchanged our vows and our rings, and she wore my mother's gold crucifix around her neck—the one I gave her when we were first together. If our wedding was incomplete, at least our love was not.

But now, I was a man with a growing family, still new to America in a time when young men were needed. I wanted more for myself and for my family, so I enlisted. It hurt my heart to leave my loving wife after such a short time together, but I did what I felt I must do. If only I had known what was to come, I would have spent every remaining moment with her.

Now that I know why she died, I see it could have all been prevented if we didn't hide our union. If we had taken the consequences then—the disapproval of her parents, the possible backlash of the Klan, alive and well in Pennsylvania during that time—perhaps we would be together now. Maybe not, but maybe we would. Her life was ruined for nothing.

When I first went off to Fort Dix, we wrote to each other almost every day. I endured the taunts of the officers and physical exhaustion, thinking I would someday come home to my wife and child. But that was never to be.

The letters stopped coming, and I did not know why. There was no confidant I could ask, not her parents or friends. She had asked me to address the letters to a separate post box than the one used by her family.

I can only speculate what the post office employees made of my letters. And I wonder where they went, those letters that never reached her. I imagine they were thrown away after she was no longer living and her deposit on the box ran out. Perhaps my letters were read by some nosy employee after her death. But no one ever contacted me. Maybe that man or woman kept the secret.

Perhaps no one cared.

I desperately wanted to leave the base and travel back to my bride. Had she stopped loving me? How could her feelings have changed so quickly? I could not understand and urgently wanted to know, but I could not leave.

So, I wrote to my brother for help. He had been there to see us wed; he knew our love was real. Weeks later, almost two months after she had died, he sent me the article from the newspaper about her death.

A deep well of pain erupted in my heart, and I could barely withstand my last week of basic training. But what could I do? I could not leave. I had signed my life away. After Fort Dix, I was sent to Texas for specialized training and later to Europe. When I finally came home after the war had ended, I came back to Deerville.

At that time, Betty had been buried for over two years. I visited her grave and wept, and I went back to the farm where I had worked.

Everything was different. Life had moved on without me… and without her. Deerville no longer felt like home, and I was a changed man from the horrors I had endured in war. I never expected this was what my homecoming would be.

Well, I retraced my steps, of course. I felt like I had nothing: no family, no money, no career, no hope. And I went to the lake, where we had shared so many moments together. In a fit of melancholy and rage at what had been taken from me, I carved an X through the heart I had once left there. Just lightly—I did not want to erase our love. I simply felt so broken and needed to express it. But I wish I hadn't done that. It pained me years later, to see it when I came back, as if I was denying or trying to diminish our love.

I will also never forgive myself for my lack of courage because I failed to tell my former employer, Betty's grandfather, about our union. He was an old man when I returned, not the spry farmer I knew, but a hollow shell crippled by loss, from age and war and family. There was no job for me, no wife, no child, and no friends.

So, I left. What else could I do? I started over in a new town. But I never, ever forgot Betty.

CHAPTER

TWENTY-ONE

Mr. Espinoza sighs, and I sense he is pretty much done with his story. If I have done the math correctly, he is over one hundred years old, and I am sure the story has been gutting for him, draining what must be an already very limited supply of energy. He doesn't tell me what happened after he left Deerville, and I don't ask, letting him decide what he wants to share.

Mr. Espinoza puts the song back on but lowers the volume a bit so we can still talk.

"It was your song, wasn't it?" I ask, knowing the answer but wanting to hear it from him.

He smiles beneath his drooping mustache. Though he has stayed in his chair for our whole talk, now he rises haltingly to his feet and shuffles over to a dresser.

"It played on our wedding day. I never married again. I looked. I knew I shouldn't spend my life pining after a ghost. I had some good times, happiness and laughter, but I never found the right woman after Betty. Would you like to see our wedding photo?"

After my enthusiastic nod, he hands me the picture frame. I take in the details of the black-and-white photograph. In their wedding finery, they look incredibly young and are grinning from ear to ear, most likely imagining their future happiness, one that will tragically never materialize.

"I recognize you! From Betty's drawings. I didn't realize until now." I flip through the photos until I come across the one with young Mr. Spencer and the chickens. Sure enough, one of the laborers in the background looks just like the groom from the picture.

He chuckles, a dry, raspy sound. I get the feeling laughter is something that has been largely missing from Mr. Espinoza's long life.

"You learned how cautious she was with her coding and the wedding. She was always worried someone would find out and force us apart, so she had to hide me in her other pictures. Her father was hard on her and would never have accepted me, but she didn't want to overtly go against his wishes. She always said it was too bad we had to live in this world rather than getting a chance at another life together, one where we were free to love each other without her parents or anyone else telling us we could not."

Ah. So that's what she meant in her coded message—the betrayal of her parents and the other life where they could be free. Perhaps I needed a code to figure out the code because I sure didn't get it before.

I flip through a few photos on my phone, stalling on the one at the lake and showing it to him.

"Oh, yes, the back of my head." He laughs again.

"What brought you back here?" I finally ask. We have shared enough secrets by now that I am emboldened to inquire.

"I thought maybe I could be buried next to my wife. It's taken quite a bit of time, money, and lawyers to prove our union, to exercise my right to this, but it's done. When I die, I will be buried by my wife, and I've ordered a headstone with both of our names. She will be Betty Bryson Espinoza for the rest of eternity. Maybe it seems like an old man's vanity, living in the past and laying claim to her when we were together such a short time. But I know our love was true, and now the rest of the world can see it, even though we will both be dead."

The goosebumps rise on my arms when I think about what he has just said. I found out about Betty from the clipping in *The Scarlet Letter*, and now Mr. Espinoza is telling me he and Betty—a disgraced but pure-hearted woman—will finally be buried next to each other in the graveyard, sharing a tombstone, just like in the book?

On a field, sable...I had to look up that final line of the novel to understand what it meant. Wow.

But I need to get back to reality, not fiction, no matter how poetic this seems.

He points to the oxygen tanks on the floor and the small pharmacy on his dresser. "I'm on my way out. I'm a year past a hundred and full of cancer." When I start offering my condolences, he holds up one hand to stop me. "I've lived a long life. I watched boys die in the war, some who had never even kissed a girl. And my beautiful bride, taken away before she could fulfill all those goals and dreams...I had my chance. I'm okay.

"When I read about her death in the newspaper, I knew she never would have killed herself. I always wondered what happened, and now I know. You've given a dying man some closure today, and I thank you for that."

He grasps my hand and squeezes it gently. There's so much emotion in that grip. I almost cry for the love that was destroyed, the lives lost, and the life which seems to have been held back by grief.

"I stopped wearing my wedding ring on my finger after I felt that too much time had passed, but I keep it on a necklace around my neck. I'd certainly like to have the ring you found, if it's not too much trouble," he says.

Even though I probably won't be able to visit again since I am leaving town, I am positive Brian, and maybe even Mr. Spencer, will be happy to visit Mr. Espinoza, to hear his recollections of Betty and their time together. I tell Mr. Espinoza this and promise that one or both of them will deliver Betty's ring.

We say our goodbyes, and I leave Briar Creek, wondering if Betty and Juan will get to hear "Moonlight Cocktail" together again.

CHAPTER

TWENTY-TWO

There is just one more piece of unfinished business for me in Deerville. I have followed Betty's clues and figured out her story, paid my debt to her and to society by giving the police my statement which will put her killer to justice, quit my job, found Betty's secret husband to give him peace, and packed my bags. We even arranged a new home for poor Luna the cat—thanks to Mrs. Winchester, to whom we just said that Evelyn had a stroke and might never get better. Again, the police can take care of all the rest.

There's only Brian left.

Only Brian. That isn't really a fitting description for my constant companion of the summer, my lone friend at a time when I had been deserted by everyone else.

We meet at the lake, of course, sitting in his truck with the windows rolled down, like usual, so we can listen to the enchanting sounds of nature without getting dirty or completely mangled by mosquitos. First, I tell him my update about Mr. Espinoza, and of course, he is excited to meet him. With his grandpa's permission, he plans to give him Betty's shoebox as well as the ring. We both know it will return to the Spencer family pretty soon anyway, all things considered.

Brian and I have shared so much with each other in the time we've had, much of it stressful or painful in some way. But there has been such a level of comfort and intimacy, and we have had some laughs throughout all of it. Still, we have never really verbalized any of this sentimental stuff I think we both feel.

When I try to articulate this and find my words a little choked, tears brimming in my eyes, I am not totally surprised by my own actions, but I am by his.

Brian leans forward in the front seat, pausing just a moment. "Is it okay if I—"

I nod, and he kisses me. It feels pure and good and right and honest. I kiss him back without any hesitation. Our lips say what our words could not express.

It is so different than that kiss with Derek, tainted by betrayal and secrecy. Our connection has been deeper than friends and different than just boyfriend and girlfriend. We are two people tethered together by more.

I know this isn't goodbye, even though I am leaving.

And it's not.

School starts a few weeks later. When I enter the doors of Cagney High on the first day of my senior year, I walk in with a smile on my face, confident in all I have done and all that I will still do someday. I feel light and free, hopeful for the year to come as well as what lies ahead.

Unlike poor Betty, I will have the chance to reach my goals in life. No one's mere words can stop me or hurt me now. I will wear Betty's story as my armor, and I have Brian metaphorically by my side. He might be a few hours away, but he is always reachable on the phone. And we are planning to apply to colleges in the same area.

Forgive, Betty wrote once. And today, on the steam in my mirror, I receive one more, and probably final, word: *Live.*

So, I will live...for myself and for Betty.

As a small publisher collaborating with an indie horror author, we make an incredible team. But we wouldn't be able to do what we so love without you. Thank you for taking the time to read
Lake of Secrets, by Cassandra O'Sullivan Sachar.

It would mean the world to us if you would take a quick moment and leave a review on any book-purchasing platform, especially our direct website, so other readers might take a chance on us too.

Also, please check out other books written by Cassandra O'Sullivan Sachar or published by Horrorsmith Publishing, which you'll find a list of next.

And don't forget to subscribe to our newsletter for the latest horror community book news and grab your free copy of
HORRORSMITH:The Magazine from our website:
www.horrorsmithpublishing.com

ALSO BY CASSANDRA O'SULLIVAN SACHAR

Close the Door
Darkness There But Something Else
Keeper of Corpses
The Hidden Diary

ALSO BY HORRORSMITH PUBLISHING

The Devil Came Down the Mountain
Still, Dark Places
Dark Things Crawl Out
What We Do in Secret
Lake of Secrets
Haint Blue
The Taste of Tiny Bones
A Light on the Bayou
Haunted Halls
Their Hearses
Three Garden Village
Hidden Children
By the Pale Light of Illuminated Bone
Angie Baby
Crepuscular

ABOUT THE AUTHOR

Cassandra O'Sullivan Sachar is a writer and associate English professor in Pennsylvania. She holds a Doctorate of Education with a Literacy Specialization from the University of Delaware and an MFA in Creative Writing with a focus on horror fiction from Wilkes University. She is the author of the Regal Summit Book Award-winning dark suspense novel Darkness There but Something More (Wicked House Publishing), the short horror story collection Keeper of Corpses and Other Dark Tales (Velox Books), the forthcoming horror novella Close the Door (Unveiling Nightmares), and the forthcoming middle-grade mystery The Hidden Diary (Tiny Terrors). Her shorter work appears in more than forty creative publications including The Horror Zine, The Stygian Lepus, Wyldblood Magazine, and Tales from the Moonlit Path. Read her work at https://cassandraosullivansachar.com.

More Titles from
HORRORSMITH PUBLISHING

AUTHOR OF WHAT WE DO IN SECRET
CHRISTINA GRAVES
STILL,
DARK
PLACES
A PSYCHOLOGICAL THRILLER NOVEL

STILL, DARK PLACES
BY CHRISTINA GRAVES

The Seven Sisters of Still Water. Missing but not forgotten. Memorialized in graveyard stone...

Nora Gray, true crime podcast host, is being called back to her hometown over a decade later by a desperate mother. Another daughter, gone. And Nora knows more than anyone realizes, more than even she remembers.

They call it Skull House, this home back in the woods, rundown, abandoned. And for as long as Nora can recall, the local kids have dared each other to climb the stairs to the top, to brave the ghost of Helaena Barker, who they say waits in the attic behind the door...

But Skull House hides more than tales of ghosts, and it clings tightly to its secrets. Nora is convinced it also holds the missing clues to the Seven Sisters' disappearances and why Nora herself woke up in a field near the house, covered in blood, all those years ago.

While Nora investigates the missing girls, will she be able to trust anyone around her? Will she even be able to trust herself?

YOUR BEDTIME
STORIES
WILL NEVER
BE THE SAME...

THE TASTE OF
TINY BONES

VINCENT HESELWOOD

THE TASTE OF TINY BONES
BY VINCENT HESELWOOD

No one knows where he came from...He's what lingers in the shadows behind you when you turn off the lights and race up the stairs...The darkness beneath the bed that keeps your feet tucked tightly under the covers...The Bogeyman...

But Evie "Creepy" Mortenson has unknowingly found a way to make him something more than what he was, something much more vicious, something much more hungry...

A simple blog post causes new nightmares to start, new fears that give him new life, and now, something is very, very wrong.

She's lost control of the monster she created, and children are starting to die.

Will she and Detective Ezra Dean find a way to stop him before he goes viral?

You thought you were afraid of the Boogeyman before...Just wait...

HAUNTED HALLS

W. A. ROBERTS

HAUNTED HALLS
BY W. A. ROBERTS

It's every mother's worst fear: Kasey's young son, Max, has gone missing. Except, Kasey is convinced he never left the house...

Under the scrutiny of local law enforcement in a town focused on her past, Kasey must navigate the hidden passageways of her home with a boyfriend she no longer knows if she can trust and a neighbor keeping something from Kasey she desperately needs to remember.

Will Kasey discover the neighborhood's secrets before it's too late and her son is lost to the house forever?

FROM THE AUTHOR OF HALLOWS EVE
WILLIAM OSWALD

HAINT BLUE

What do you do if the Boo Hag is already inside?

HAINT BLUE
BY WILLIAM OSWALD

When their father commits suicide, Louis Lattimore and his sister, Ruby, are forced to move across the country at the behest of their mother, to a secret family estate tucked away among the sea islands of South Carolina.

Louis is soon befriended by his two new neighbors and learns his new home is nothing like his old one in upstate New York. But it's not just culture shock Louis is wrestling. The locals seem convinced the family mansion is haunted.

According to the local Gullah people, the manor is possessed by an insatiable spirit dubbed the Boo-hag. At the insistence of his new friends, Louis reluctantly seeks help from Auntie Caroline, an elderly member of the Gullah community revered to an almost supernatural status, and with good reason.

Is she the only person who can help save Louis and Ruby from the Boo-hag?

HUSHED HORROR SERIES BOOK ONE

THE STILL

BELLA DEAN JOYNER

THE STILL
BY BELLA DEAN JOYNER

Lana Wellington and Derek Armary individually find themselves seeking fresh starts in Edelleen, Colorado, located along the calm banks of the South Platte River. But within the shadows of the town's historic mill, something evil stirs, something vengeful.

When the first dead body is discovered in the woods, followed by a second, Sheriff Curtis Haines believes he's on the trail of a serial killer. But by the time his own deputies begin to report sightings of a strange, robed figure, Haines remembers rumors of a decades-old murder and wonders if something more supernatural has fallen upon Edelleen.

With a failing marriage and small-town politics hampering his efforts, Haines leans heavily on the rest of the force and the citizens to find answers about what happened at the old mill all those years ago.

The creature crawling from the stagnant waters near the old mill has set its sights on Lana and Derek, who now must help Haines figure out who or what is responsible for calling it forth into Edelleen, and why.

But will they die trying?

A. A. PFAU

CREPUSCULAR

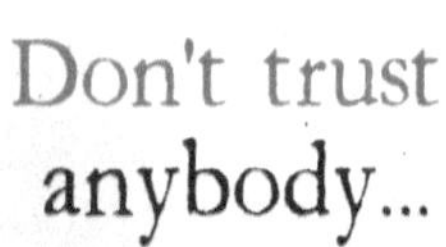

Don't trust
anybody...

CREPUSCULAR
BY A. A. PFAU

Thirteen-year-old Dylan Fisher and his classmates are returning to their sleepy coastal town after a week-long camp and an abnormal summer storm.

But before they even make it back into town, something stops them in the road.

Something hungry...

Knowing the bus is no longer safe, the teens attempt to make it back into town on foot, only to find everything deserted. Their loved ones are gone.

Or are they?

Don't trust anybody...